the Red Shirt

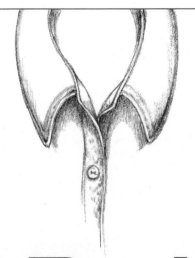

theRed Shirt

A novel by
Lois Leardi

DELPHINIUM BOOKS
harrison, new york   encino, california

Copyright © 1991 by Lois Leardi

Library of Congress Cataloging-in-Publication Data
Leardi, Lois, 1954–
The red shirt : a novel / by Lois Leardi.—1st ed.
p. cm.
ISBN 0-671-74259-0 : $18.95
I. Title.
PS3562.E239R4   1990
813'.54—dc20   91-16269
CIP

First Edition   All rights reserved
10 9 8 7 6 5 4 3 2 1

Published by Delphinium Books, Inc.
20 Pleasant Ridge Road
Harrison, N.Y. 10528

Distributed by Simon & Schuster
Printed in the United States of America

Jacket art by Milton Charles
Text design by Milton Charles
Production services by Blaze International Productions, Inc.

Lyrics on pages 31–32 are from "Candy Man Blues",
words and music by John Hurt, copyright © 1963
by Wynwood Music Co., Inc. All rights reserved.
Used by permission.

For
Larry
and
Lila

Chapter One
The Red Shirt

The Red Shirt

A woman was standing in her father's garden keeping silent. Looking at her, it would seem as if she had been standing that way for years, the seasons and the silence settling over her, peeling back the layers of her flesh until she appeared mottled, worn down, made of porous rock like the chalky limestone madonnas that stand chipped and crumbling in gardens all over the world. To the south was Manhattan, to the north, Poughkeepsie. She had seen neither. Her life had taken place on a small stretch of riverbank spattered with train yard cinders, dipping down to the oily black Hudson. She had occupied no more than the four tiny rooms of her father's house, with its goat shed behind it and its tired garden on the hillside above. She had cloistered herself so long ago that she could not remember the beginning of her silence, not the first hours, nor the first days, nor how it had gathered momentum, turning into a week, a month, now more than three months. A conflict had started, somewhere in school, something that had sent her racing home, swinging at the goats who had bounded to meet her, their docile heads bent in confusion. Now she could not remember, except to imagine that it had been, perhaps, nothing more than the slow, sad welling up of pain.

Now she was going to speak. She must.

Twilight was drawing its rattan shade over the riverbank. The air was cool, the earth still warm. Light filtered here and there. The last slice of sun hung on the mountains of the western shore. The river had gone completely black. Hannah stood, waiting for her father.

This would be one of the last times, she told herself, that she would wait for him. She was going to speak, and then she was going to leave.

She wondered how it would be. She pictured herself moving out into that vast space of the world, with her dull, flat face, her tongue thick with disuse, her defeated shoulders and large, nervous hands—looking for work. I know how to milk goats, she would say, and I know how to wait.

She would hold herself tightly, she decided, and not let the world sniff her sad, fermented core. She would defy what was out there.

Such thinking, she knew, was a lie. In reality she was terrified. When she thought of living out in the world she most often pictured herself lying alone in a rented room, on a soiled, lumpy mattress, shivering with fear, maybe sick, fevered, dying.

Still, she would go. She did not blame her father. He had not told her to keep silent, nor to stay at home. In fact Jackson had protected her, slamming down the phone on school officials, on the psychologist and the social worker. She is old enough to quit school, he had argued. She is old enough to do as she pleases.

The silence had just begun. Jackson was not to blame.

Why then, she wondered, did she hate him now?

Hannah looked about the garden and sat down, patting the earth with her palm. The last shadows stretched tall, leaning up the hillside to the house. It was a fragile house, thin and sad, with crooked windows and mismatched doors and a black tarred roof. Jackson had built it from scraps one summer before she was born. It was, she thought, the kind of thing folksingers did. It was the kind of house that went with the deep dismal thump of her father's guitar in blues time.

Jackson had not, as he had hoped, become famous. He had spent most nights playing on street corners in New York, a cigar box open at his feet. He had done this all through her childhood, shuttling back on the train at night, rising to go to his job in the factory in the morning. He played the bars and coffeehouses that lined the Hudson, and he was worn down with it now, like a stone that has lain deep in the river, rounding itself, riddled with pits and pores. Hannah did not know what made him continue to sing, the angry shoulders of his red shirt hunched over the box of the old Martin, his yellow thumb smacking the bass string, his throat jerking down the whiskey.

There had been the absence of her mother. For as long as she could remember, Hannah had looked for her. There had been times, deep in the night, when the kitchen door would bang back and chaotic music would fill the house as the guitar cracked against the table edge, and Hannah would come out into the cold kitchen to unlace his workshoes, always looking to the door for the miracle of her, for Patience, her mother.

Hannah crossed her arms over her chest and breathed deeply. The river was glorious. The last of the light hung in points, surrounding a string of barges. A single column of smoke rose. Everything was quiet. It was going to happen now. She was going to speak.

It had been almost four months, and, for a second, she imagined her voice twisted and deformed, perhaps nonexistent.

She bit her lip.

"Juh," she said, and then, "Jackson."

Her voice was good.

Suddenly on the road below she saw the flash of her father's red shirt through the trees.

※

Hannah had believed for several years that had she been raised in a church she would have made a fine nun, and now, with her father's name still on her tongue, she longed for something religious to do. She reached behind her and snatched a dead cornstalk, clasping it like a shepherd's rod.

She came down the hill.

Jackson stepped into the clearing just as the light dipped below the mountains. He was limping. The red shirt flapped open. His chest below had sunk into a hollow around his breastbone, ribs and clavicle jutting out. His skin gleamed with fever. The whiskey flask, almost half empty, hung in the crook of his forefinger. His eyes watched her. He seemed pleased that she had come to greet him, as she so often did.

Just then he seemed fragile. It was as if his bones could be heard creaking beneath his flesh. His hands, his feet, his sex, all seemed worn down. Hannah stood before him, grasping the cornstalk, and studied the purple fever sores that dotted his lip.

He was rotting. Something was eating him.

Yet he was strangely calm. It occurred to Hannah then that Jackson knew, after weeks of bending over her anxiously each evening, that this evening was different. Just as she was watching something eat him, he had, all along, been watching something eat her. And, because of this, he had begun to smile, so that part of his lip burst and bubbled with blood.

He said nothing.

Hannah swallowed. Jackson lifted his hand and touched her shoulder.

"Jackson," she said. "Jackson, it's me."

And Jackson, tilting his head as if listening to music, began to laugh. Hannah began to laugh with him. They walked up the hillside toward the house, leaning into one another. Jackson offered Hannah the whiskey, and she drank, scorching her throat.

౽

They became drunk. They sat across from one another at the table, passing the flask, ignoring the supper she had prepared, and the goats who bleated impatiently at the back door, their teats swollen with the evening milk.

"I knew you would talk again," he said.

Hannah took the whiskey. She made fists under the table.

"Makes you feel pretty good, don't it?" he asked.

He watched her eagerly, his eyes egging her on.

And Hannah thought, in that single passing moment, that she might lift the bottle and send it crashing into his face. She did not know where this anger came from, but it caused her to lean over the table, her face close to his as she spoke.

"Jackson," she said. "I'm leaving you."

He started. He coughed.

And Hannah, weakening, folded her hands to keep from reaching across to him. His hair hung in long greasy strands, matted with sweat. She wanted to tuck it back behind his ears, to fetch a cool washcloth. He spat into a handkerchief.

"You ought to go to a doctor," she said.

Jackson looked away. His face had grown gaunt, so that the skin of his nose appeared ready to split.

"Where are you going?" he asked.

"I'm going everywhere," she answered.

Jackson laughed. He pushed back his chair and stood up. The armpits of his red shirt were black with sweat.

"Everywhere!" he said.

"Don't laugh, Jackson," she said.

She stood up suddenly and began moving about the room. The wooden floorboards creaked beneath her feet. She swung at the copper pots that hung from the beams, and at the woodbox, and the shelves lined with oilcloth. She swung in circles around Jackson, who crossed his rail-like arms over his chest, coughing.

"I'm sick of it here!" she hissed. "I'm sick of you!"

Jackson looked away.

"I've been waiting and waiting—"

"For what?" Jackson asked.

And Hannah, her arm raised, stopped suddenly, so that her knees felt as if they were shattering at the joints, and she reached for a chair. Her breath came in like an injection, and puffed out the way a child sighs after a long time of crying.

"I'm sorry," she said.

Jackson was coughing.

"It's not like you told me to stay," she said.

"No," he coughed. "It ain't."

"It's just that, Jackson, well—don't you want more?"

Jackson laughed bitterly. He ran his fingers through his hair.

"Honey," he said sadly, "if you want more, then you go and get more. Nobody's keeping you."

Hannah reached and took the bottle from his hand.

"We're drunk," she said. She looked her father up and down, her eyes resting on his workshoes.

"When's the last time you made love, Jackson?" she asked.

Jackson did not answer her. The kerosene lamp began to sputter and he leaned over and adjusted the wick.

He began to tap his foot.

Hannah raised her eyes and saw him staring at her.

The Red Shirt

"Tell me about Patience," she said.

Jackson said, "Your mother was a whore.

"Don't look so startled. If you're going to talk now, and go out on your own, then I'll tell you this story so that when you see a whore on the street with her shoulders shoved back into the wall of a building, you'll know—well, never mind—give me the bottle—you'll think as you please.

"She came into a bar I was playing in New York one night. That was more than twenty years ago now. I doubt the place is even there anymore. She came in, and I wanted her, so when I collected my pay at the end of the gig I flashed it under her nose, and she just laughed and walked out like she was insulted. I had to have her then. I trotted down the street after her and I said, Please, Miss, let me buy you a cup of coffee. Her eyes got round when I called her Miss. She stopped in the street, your mother, and she turned and looked me right in the eye. If you want it that bad, she said, you can pay me the rest on time. I'll expect interest though.

"I began to buy Patience regularly, and it wasn't long before I owed her thousands of dollars. I spent every Friday and Saturday night in her room, and she was losing business. She'd keep reminding me about the money, writing down sums on scraps of paper, but something was beginning to happen to us, between the eyes, and after awhile we stopped mentioning money altogether. Then one night I found her on the bed with her face all smashed.

"So I brought her here. I was in love with her. I didn't know she was a con artist. I thought I had saved her. I thought I had brought her up from a life on the street and she would be grateful to me. It's such an old story. Everyone knows this story. Even if I don't tell you the rest of it, you know it. You know what happened to your mother. She was a whore.

"There must be another half pint. Look under the sink.

"I begged her to have a child. I was desperate to keep her. She didn't love me. She was biding time all through that pregnancy. God knows how many children she's had. From the way she turned her nose up at you, I figured you weren't the first. She carried you like you were a stone. She let you cry for hours on end. You choked on canned formula for weeks, but she wouldn't touch you to her breast. You had cradle cap and diaper rash, and God knows what else between your little fingers and toes.

"I let it pass. I said, Give her time to get used to this.

"She wouldn't name you. For a long time you had no name at all, and it wasn't until just before she left that I was singing an old blues, one night, the one that says Go Down Old Hannah, and I named you Hannah, after the sun. It took you a long time to figure out that you had a name.

"She left exactly on your first birthday. I came home from the factory with a cake and a pound of fresh coffee and I found you locked in the bedroom closet. When I opened the door you screamed and wouldn't let me touch you. You kept circling around the house like you were looking for her, until you exhausted yourself, and then you slept all the way through the night for the first time in your life. I sat up in the kitchen and towards morning I put my fist through the window and cut my hand pretty bad.

"Four days later I called the County Welfare and told them I had a kid to get rid of. They sent a man out here. I told him you were keeping me out of work and I couldn't afford a housekeeper. He said, 'Get her things together and I'll take her right now.' I started throwing all your things into a paper bag and you were watching me and you came over and threw your bottle into the bag and laughed like it was a game.

"But you screamed all the way out to the car. That guy had three baby seats lined up in the back. I felt like I was turning you over to a dog catcher. He strapped you in, and you were screaming, and I said, take her out, I changed my mind.

"He gave me the name of Linda Mason, and she watched you and about six other babies in her basement every week for the next five years. You remember her? I left you with Linda most nights when I went out to play music. We had an affair, but nothing ever came of it. I lost track of her once you started school.

"I was mad at you most of the time. You grew up to be the spitting image of Patience, and that wasn't easy. Once I threw you down the back steps for no other reason, when you were about thirteen, and I know you never forgot that."

Jackson wiped the back of his hand over his mouth and some of the skin on his lips tore loose. Hannah sat across from him, barely moving. After a long time she got up and went out to the goats.

It was midnight when Jackson got out the guitar, pressing it under his chin, pulling out his Barlow knife so that he could slide the blade over the shining strings. It made a blurred sound as he played, his thumb smacking out a drunken rhythm. He had pushed a candle into the grain of the wooden table, and as he played Hannah sat in the shadows, one bare heel ticking against the rung of her chair.

How easy it would be, she thought, to murder him. It was only a matter of wresting the Barlow knife from him and plunging it, hard and fast, between his gaping ribs, then dragging it, crosswise, ripping him open. He would scream a terrified scream that would gurgle as his lungs were bloated with blood. His eyes would search hers for only a second before they glazed over with the knowledge of his own death, rolling up as he thought his very last thought. And what would that be? A memory? The image of a person? A last emotion? Hate? Fear? What does terror think? Perhaps, she thought, the brain has an electrical storm of uncontrollable images. Perhaps he would flash all the way back to his infancy, remember his mother, remember something like the smell of hair that has been stroked down greasy and flat; and then Jackson's body would slump, and he would be dead.

❦

Two weeks ago Jackson had brought a young man into the house. He stood in the doorway, gawking, clutching a fiddlebox, his eyes blinking wetly behind rimless spectacles. He had a tangle of yellow curls knotted at his neck with a rubber band. He wore jeans that hung low over jutting hipbones, his sex nestling in the whitened crotch. His legs bowed at the knees. He called himself Frisco. He was, Jackson declared, hungry, and would she find him something to eat? She don't talk, Jackson said, but she cooks well enough, and the young man had looked away, flushing, shuffling his feet.

For two weeks they had watched one another, not speaking. She knew nothing about him save for the energetic scratch of his fiddle strings, deep in the night, beyond her bedroom doorway. She served him tea with averted eyes. She knew the back of him more intimately than the front, the shrug of his shoulders, the crease that separated his high, rounded buttocks, the turned heels of his heavy hiking boots.

He was the only person besides Jackson that she had seen all summer.

His eyes followed Jackson with the love of a disciple. He said little. He was a poor lost boy with large hands, nervous, perhaps a virgin. He played mechanically, stumbling behind Jackson who went on ahead, calling out notes to him which he scampered to find, the sweat beading on his upper lip.

He seemed incapable of anger or impatience.

There was a certain fear in him. He moved as if he expected at any moment to be struck, and he often smiled to himself, making him look simple or dull. He had his own world, as Hannah had hers. He could sit for an hour over a cup of tea. For this Hannah was afraid of him, and attracted to him as well.

Now he was coming up the hill. He kept his eyes to the ground, while all around him leaves spun and dropped and the moon hung full over the river. He walked with his toes turned in, comforting himself in some way. His hiking boots played with the surface of each rock. Halfway to the house he paused, raising his head to sniff the air.

"Jackson," she said, addressing the kitchen wall, "Frisco is coming up the path."

She heard the whiskey flask settle on the floor beside the bathtub.

"Run and invite him in!" Jackson called. "Tell him you're talking!"

He laughed.

Hannah shuddered. She did not want to talk to Frisco. She did not want him looking at her. She did not want to ruin all the watching they had done, all the looking quickly away, all the ignoring that had kept the presence of one another safe and controlled and attractive. Words with Frisco, she believed, would make her ugly, no longer a mystery, only a brittle, starving old girl that Frisco would turn from.

She was suddenly frightened. As Frisco resumed his walk up the hill, Hannah skimmed over the back steps and ran to the goat shed.

෴

It was dark in the shed. She lit a lamp and began casting about for something to do. The goats had already settled themselves, and now they lifted their heads and bleated. Hannah shushed them and began to sweep. She poked at the dirt floor. Twenty minutes passed. His presence in the doorframe made the kerosene lamps sputter. He was holding two steaming mugs and gazing at some point directly above her.

"I've brought you some tea," he whispered.

She stopped sweeping.

"Your father said," he swallowed. "He said that you were talking."

Shadows flickered in the rafters.

"Yes," she said.

"It's got honey in it," he offered.

They sat in the hay.

"I didn't know you could talk," Frisco said.

They looked away, she at the pen gate, and he at the doorway.

"Will you come with us to the cafe tonight?" he asked.

Hannah turned. Frisco leaned toward her.

"I know it's been months since you were away from the house, but, I was thinking, since it's only down to Boone's, that if you wanted to leave I could take you back in the truck."

He looked away.

She closed her eyes.

"Anyway," he added limply, "Jackson's looking for his red shirt."

"I laid it up in the garden to dry," she said.

She got up.

"Will you come?" he asked.

"Yes," she said slowly. "I will."

She rode in the truck. Jackson settled her at a table in Boone's Cafe. He pressed a cold bottle of beer between her palms. For a moment he squatted beside her, taking whiskey from a mason jar.

"It's all right," he said.

Then he went away.

The room would not focus for a moment.

She had almost forgotten what people looked like.

She remembered that when she had left the world they had all been liars, and they had all been angry, and her father in his red shirt had stood angry behind his guitar while Hannah smoothed a miniskirt over her nervous thighs and lockers slammed and a girl she had played with years ago walked past her in the library and whispered: "Your father's a damn radical." The senior ring and the senior prom were being discussed by doves and hawks alike, and one day it had simply ceased to have any meaning at all, and so she had straightened out her locker and gone home. In the cafe she realized that she was still haunted by the fact that behind each pair of eyes was a sensitive area, wanting something it could not name. And so she looked down and away from them all and thought: Soon I will be out here too, alone, and it will not be very different from the life I have led with Jackson, not lonelier, not less lonely, and for all I know, pointless.

Still she was going. She hooked her workshoes into the rungs of her chair and turned her attention to Jackson.

He sat on a wooden stool, leaning forward, the mason jar resting on the floor at his feet. From time to time he would glance up and turn his face from the microphone and cough. The rolled sleeves of his red shirt made black hollows around his skinny arms. His temples were blue. His eyes, shadowed by the single bulb above him, were sunken. His brow and nose and cheekbones were a startling shade of green, pushing through his skin as if he were moulding from beneath. All around him cigarette smoke rose, glasses clinked, sirens rang out from a television above the bar, a toilet flushed. Hannah had raised the beer halfway to her lips when it became clear to her, for the first time, that Jackson was really dying.

He was dying.

She ran.

Before her the river sprawled in the moonlight, its black waves rippling like the fur of some great prehistoric animal, huge and lumbering and hungry.

I've killed him, she thought. I've grown up to look like Patience, and together Patience and I have killed him.

Hannah squatted in the dust and watched the river. The Hudson was wider here. It was a different view and it could have been a different river, so unlike the one she had lived with all summer.

There was so much to tell him.

Jackson, she would say, I remember lying at the bottom of those stairs. I kept my face to the flagstones, wishing for blood. I prayed that you had paralyzed me. I prayed that you would spend the rest of your life bending over me, pushing me about, lifting me from bed to wheelchair, guilty. When I knew I was not hurt I lay still and waited for you to come down and pick me up. I waited to forgive you, but you only stood in the doorway, and when I raised my head you turned and I heard the rattle of ice cubes.

I wanted you.

When I was thirteen I used to pretend that you and I were Africans, and that we lived on the banks of a great river, deep in the jungle, and that there was danger around us all the time. I used to pretend that you were my protector, my man, and that, were it not for you, I could die at any time. You stood between me and the jungle, and I cowered behind you. I used to stand at the sink, kneading your red shirt with suds, and in my mind's eye you were just around the bend in the tracks, squatting in the center of our village, tossing the gambling stones, your mouth parted in triumph, your yellow teeth whistling victory. At night, when you ducked through the doorway I would breathe the hot smell of the forest and feel safe. At thirteen, Jackson, I slept with my rag doll, and I would lie her across my stomach and pretend that she was our child.

When I got up from the bottom of those stairs I knew that you had the power to hurt me, and I knew that I wanted, more than anything, to punish you with my own pain. I did not know that five years later I would stop talking. I did not know that five years later you would be dying.

She was sorry now. Jackson was going to die and leave her, and she was not going to be able to leave him. She was going to be punished.

She wanted him to come, but it was Frisco, his hiking

boots striking the cinders, who leaned behind her. "Are you all right?" he asked.

Hannah traced in the dust with a stick.

Frisco pulled his spectacles off and then put them back on.

"Is it the people? Is it too much for you? I'll take you home."

"No," she said.

The tide was shifting. The air smelled of salt. Hannah sat down in the space where the road left off and turned to dirt. She plucked a blade of grass that was thick with train yard soot. It was very dark.

"You shouldn't have come," Frisco said. "It was too soon for you. It was my fault. I'm sorry."

"Don't be a fool," she said.

Frisco glanced nervously toward the cafe. He sat down, jerking up his knees.

"Richard O'Connor is in there," he said.

Hannah looked closely at Frisco. He pushed his spectacles up.

"He's an agent. A good one."

"He's in there now?" she asked.

"He wants to make a tape."

Hannah spun around and got up on her knees.

"Now?" she asked.

Frisco nodded. He looked out over the river, away from her.

"Jackson is dying," she said.

Frisco was startled. His profile in the darkness was that of an old boy, the cheekbones etched in simple wisdom, as if he understood stillness and quiet completely. Hannah thought then that whatever Frisco had seen, whatever he had heard and known and lived through remained locked in this simplicity, buried in his childishness. He was a man still reeling from the time before words and power, from the time when everything affected him and he affected nothing. She could see then that Frisco understood that it was all beyond his control, and that to control it, though it might make him a man, would not make him happy. And so it was very wistful: his face, his yellow curls, the black river.

"He's very sick," Frisco said quietly.
Hannah closed her eyes. A train whistle blew from far upriver.
"What is it?" she asked.
Frisco tapped his knee.
"His lungs," he said.
Hannah opened her eyes.
"I'm going down to the water now," she said. "You can go back and finish the gig."
She stood up. Frisco stood also.
"It's Jackson's gig," he said. "No one in there is listening to me."
They stepped over the tracks and picked their way through reeds and cattails, long dead. Tonight would mark the first real frost, she was sure of it. Frisco walked beside her, silent, nervous, embarrassed by his own presence. The riverbank was rocky here. She felt disoriented, dizzy, frightened by the strange landscape. She stood very still, and when Frisco came up behind her she reached and took his hand. His palm

was wet, skittish. She heard him swallow in the darkness. She was angry with him suddenly. She wanted to turn on him, slap him into someone strong, someone who could hold her, someone she could press up against and be comforted by. Instead his wet hand was gripping hers and she wanted to wrench away from him. She wanted, in some vague way, to fling herself into the freezing river, to be done with them both, these two men who stood so weak and impotent in her life. With the end of silence she wanted to end all that was pent up and unexpressed. She hated him in this moment, this overgrown boy who plodded after Jackson like a blind puppy still wet with afterbirth. Yet she held his hand and listened to him swallow. Where had he been, she wondered, and where had he come from, and why had he stayed, these two weeks, and where did he live, and what did he do in all the hours that he was not at the house mooning around Jackson, clutching his warped old fiddle as if it were made of gold? What words trembled on Frisco's lips, deep in the night, when he lay in his bed, wherever it was, fearing death? How long had he known about Jackson; how long had the two of them known and conspired not to tell—how long had she known herself, watching each evening, denying, pretending her father was only tired, while the fever licked at his wasted flesh and the coughing, oh God, the coughing pierced deeper and deeper until she had believed he was coughing up his very insides? Each evening this boy had come, his boots clattering over the flagstones, his eyes brimming with love, his throat trembling with what he was not saying, taking tea from her with a nod of thanks, receiving her silence with his uncertainty, looking away, knowing that Jackson was dying.

Now she held his hand. He clawed at his dense curls for a moment, and then, as if reaching for something he would be hit for, he touched her face. Hannah stood like a stone as he traced the frozen passage of her brow, smudging her eyelid with his leathery thumb.

"It's cold," she said.

Frisco continued to stare.

"I'm going back," she said, and she turned, leaving his hand dangling in the air. She started over the train tracks. When she looked behind her he was still standing at the river. He was tiny in all that empty blackness. He stood with his shoulders hunched, his hands hidden now in his armpits. His hair blew in silver knots all around his child's face, and his toes curled inward over the rocks.

In the morning she sat in the goat shed with her knees flung wide around the milking pail, grasping a swollen teat in each fist. Hannah pressed her face into the scratchy flank of the gray goat and breathed the smell of morning. Beyond the shed doorway the world sat in meditation, transformed by the first hoarfrost. Grass and garden and house and river hung suspended in softness, sun licked and radiant.

It was late. Jackson had not yet appeared. His lunch pail lay on the back stoop, where she left it each morning, his workshoes sagging beside it. Was he still sleeping? Hannah grasped the handle of the pail and hefted it to her hip.

He could be dead.

She eyed the back door of the house.

He could be lying in there dead, twisted stiff in the folds of his quilt, his face dusted with frost.

She walked barefoot over the frozen earth, sloshing the hot milk which hissed as it struck the ground. She walked down the slope, sliding over the rocks, splashing through the little creek that burned her feet with its iciness.

Jackson: Don't be dead.

If she had religion, now, she could cross herself and make a bargain. Dear God, if you let him live, just this once, I will never do whatever it is that I do that offends you again.

She paused at the back steps. The woods were so still. She could smell the coffee she had burned earlier, and could smell the smell of the house, that timeless odor of old boards and rotting linoleum.

She went up and set the pail on the doorstep. The kitchen was dark and cold. The coffeepot sputtered on the stove. A pale light filtered through the dirty window and fell across his naked shoulder blades. Jackson sat hunched over the table, coughing, scratching furiously on a piece of paper with an old pencil stub. She closed her eyes for a second and breathed.

"You ought to have a shirt on," she said.

He said nothing.

Hannah brought the milk in and began pouring it through a funnel into jars.

"Aren't you going to work?"

Jackson stopped writing. He flicked his long hair back. His temples were blue.

"I thought I'd take the day off."

Hannah poured a cup of coffee and sat down across from him. She lifted a rank smelling sweater from a nail behind her and extended it. Their eyes met, Jackson's red rimmed, sunken darkly in his face. He pulled the sweater on. His wrists poked from the frayed cuffs. She could see the veins pulsing there, running like rivers along the edge of each thumb.

He crumpled the paper he had been writing on.

"First frost," he remarked.

"Tell me about Richard O'Connor," she said.

Jackson looked up.

"How do you know about him?"

Hannah did not answer.

Jackson stood up. He kept his hand on the table for a moment, steadying himself. He coughed once. He poured himself coffee at the stove and Hannah watched the back of him. She watched the nape of his neck where his dark hair lay sweat-soaked and matted. He seemed so vulnerable there, so tender, so close to the surface that she wanted to go and lay her lips at the base of his skull, cooling his restless fever.

"Well," Jackson began slowly. He sipped the coffee, set it down, rummaged in the empty sugar pot. "He says that about two years ago he got a tip from a friend who'd heard me one night down at the Redneck—Jesus, of all places—and so then he came and heard me himself, maybe a year ago, at Boone's, and he was impressed, but not ready to do anything. Now, he says, I've grown into it. Now, he says, I'm doing what he wants. I told him, forget it, I'm fifty years old. He said, too old for your own TV special, but I somehow don't think that's what you're after. We laughed. He said, You're doing something important. So he wants to tape a little, just something casual, and hang out with it for awhile. He says Recipe might be interested." Jackson paused and blinked his eyes. "He's an agent. He's slick. But I like him."

Hannah smiled carefully.

"Richard O'Connor is a fine man," Jackson said, "but he should've come around ten or twenty years ago."

And the corners of Jackson's mouth trembled.

"Don't we have any sugar?" he asked.

Hannah lowered her eyes.

"Jackson," she said, "I know about the cancer. I know that you are dying."

Jackson stood very still, cradling the sugar pot in the palm of his hand. The veins in his temples worked. He looked small, self-conscious, frightened. For a long moment Hannah looked at him as if he were only a man, trapped in the murderous uprising of his own body, and not her father—just someone alone, worn to the marrow, someone not feeling well and knowing that he would never feel well again. And what she saw was not so much his despair as his embarrassment.

Jackson looked away toward the back door. He studied the calico curtains that hung stiff with kitchen grease.

"Don't be angry with Frisco," she said. "I saw it before he came out after me." She stuck her hands roughly into the pockets of her overalls. "I've been seeing it for a long time. I just haven't let myself know what I was seeing."

Jackson bristled. He hunched one shoulder as if it pained him. She wondered for a moment if he was crying, and her heart began to pound.

"Have you been to the hospital?"

He said nothing. He took a sip of coffee and she watched his neck strain to swallow it.

"Please, Jackson," she said. "I need to know."

Jackson looked up. She watched his eyes travel over her face and she felt herself harden like rock. She knew that in this instant she was beautiful to Jackson, that he loved her, and she pushed it away with her flat face, frightened of what was so strong between them, frightened that Patience was not there to interrupt, frightened that right now she *was* Patience, frightened that someone so dead, dying, rotting, could be so hungry, could arouse her so. She felt her eyes flit nervously to one side. She glanced down, startled to see that he had extended his cup, and she fumbled with the coffeepot. Jackson reached out and touched the collar of her workshirt, folding it over.

"There ain't anything I can tell you," he said, "that you can't see." He crossed the room to the window. "Six months ago they told me I could have surgery, but that the cancer was all through my chest. They told me my liver's messed up. They wanted me to have chemotherapy." He drummed his fingers on the windowpane. "They said maybe a year ago they could have done something for me." He pushed his hair back. "I ran myself down," he said.

He did not sound sorry. He only sounded tired.

"What do they say now?" she asked.

Jackson looked over his shoulder at her. His face was calm, almost blank.

"They're real polite. They smile and say, There's a chance, Mr. Spencer. Miracles happen. They don't say what any fool can see." He lifted his head and snorted. "My God, Hannah, even the goats know. They skit away from me like I've been dead a week already."

Hannah lowered her eyes. She prodded herself for something to say, something that would break the hardness in his eyes and comfort him. That was what speaking people did, she told herself. They searched, constantly, for the right thing to say. She raked the floor with her toe.

"Maybe there's a chance," she said. "This thing with Richard O'Connor could be it. He's made the first serious offer you've ever had. Maybe if you did that chemotherapy, knowing that you really had something to live for, you could make it. You could get well."

Jackson coughed.

"I can't do both," he said hoarsely.

Hannah bit her lip and looked carefully at him. Why had he waited so long? Perhaps he never knew he was sick. Maybe death had snuck up imperceptibly, like a cat prowling unseen in the dark, unnoticed because Jackson had been so dark for so long that no light could have filtered in.

"I didn't want you to know," he said. "I guess something in me was hoping that after all these weeks you were going to talk, and to fly on out of here before you ever knew. I should have got you help. I should have got you to a doctor, a hospital, someplace." His hands were shaking. "Look, Hannah, I'll give you all the money I have. Don't stick around for this. If I could stay around any longer and do anything to help you, you know I would."

His eyes strayed to the whiskey bottle on the windowsill. He reached and unscrewed the cap. He rubbed the label with his thumb.

"I'm going to work with Richard," he said.

Hannah came silently and stood behind him. Her arms ached. She wanted, more than anything, to gather his thick brown hair between her palms.

"I'm not going to leave," she said. "I'm going to stay here with you."

She touched his shoulder. Jackson took a long drink, and as he swallowed he allowed his head to drop until his cheek rested on the back of her hand.

Time passed. Snow fell. The edges of the river rose up in thick gray slabs. The earth was sharp, frozen into ridges and gullies that snagged at the soles of her shoes, and Hannah, walking from the shed one evening, wondered how they would ever dig a grave in this unyielding earth.

Lamplight flickered at the back door. She breathed the smoke which lay on the air like a musty quilt. Christmas had passed; still Jackson lived, mostly by the stove door, hugging the guitar, coughing songs into Richard O'Connor's elaborate machine. Frisco came each morning now. His face was growing long and hard. His eyes were older, they traveled over

Jackson with new distance, over Hannah with new intensity. He stood behind Jackson, the fiddle jutting from his neck, sawing the strings with a gravity that frightened her.

She could not understand why Richard continued to come, lugging his machine up the back steps, leaning over her father as if Jackson were an oracle he had come to consult. Once more, he would urge, and Jackson, smiling like a Halloween skeleton, would begin, for the fifth or sixth time, some ragged old blues she had heard all her life.

Why were they all dreaming? Did they think that Jackson was going to live to make record albums? Did Richard think that he had stumbled upon a great artist? Who was Jackson? Jackson was no one! Jackson was a fool who had lived a fool's life, a dreamer, a drinker, an angry father, a forlorn lover. Jackson had been dying since the day Patience had left. He was no artist. He was no courageous being. How could they listen, these men, to the incessant aching that never ended with him?

Hannah pulled her jacket tighter. She kicked the ground. She went inside.

Without looking up, Richard motioned for her to be quiet. She pulled the door carefully shut and tip-toed over the creaking floor. Jackson huddled in his chair, singing into the microphone, his shoulder blades working furiously over the guitar, his foot tapping against the hearth. Frisco scratched and squealed on the fiddle behind him, the hairs snapping and flying from his bow. They were all sweating. Richard scurried to control the knobs and meters of his machine. The room was hot. The single kitchen window was steamed over. Hannah hoisted herself up on the wooden counter and smudged her finger idly through a line of honey that had dribbled over the edge.

She had decided, some time ago, that Richard was beautiful. He came into the house each evening dressed in tweed and cashmere, his hair shining like silk, his face shaven so close that it looked like wax. Hannah watched him, and as she did she could see Frisco staring at her from the corner of her eye. She could see his face reddening, his lips parting, his attention straying from the fiddle. She looked quickly away from Richard just as Frisco drew a wrong note, and they all stopped, Richard throwing up his hands in disgust, Jackson kicking the stove door. Frisco lowered his eyes, blushing, and backed away.

Jackson began to tune the guitar. Hannah poured Richard a cup of tea and he took it from her. Jackson took tea also. He was tired and far away and he held her wrist for a moment before letting it go.

"Sing a song with me," he said.

Hannah hesitated.

"Just this once," Jackson said.

She squatted down beside the chair. Richard pressed a button and Jackson began to sing, so soft and low that she had to tilt her head to hear. It was an old, old song. It was a song she had heard deep in the night all her life:

> All you ladies, gather round,
> The good sweet candy man's in town.

Hannah drew a breath and touched her hand to her throat. Her voice, blending into his, was timid, trembling, and so strangely like his that they seemed to be one voice:

> Don't stand close to the candy man,
> He'll ease a stick of candy in your hand.

And here her father's voice cracked, rolling into a thick rattle that doubled him over with coughing so wretched that she pulled the guitar from him and braced his forehead with her hands.

In the morning she rose and sifted flour. The house was cold, the fire nearly out. The windowpanes were frosted with ice, and through them the river made a black gash across the landscape. She stirred flapjack batter, balancing the bowl on her hip as she stood near the stove. The house was very quiet. She wished suddenly for cats, lots of them curling on the windowsills and stretching against her leg, mewing for milk, knocking over the plants which were dead now, unable to bear the cold of the house. The heat was coming slowly. She set a tin of maple syrup on the wood stove, warming it for Jackson.

An hour passed, and then another. She became uneasy. She boiled water and stirred molasses in it. She took it to his bedroom doorway. She could hear him breathing. The door was ajar. She could see the long blue line of his arm resting across his stomach. The quilt rose and fell with a halting, uneven rhythm.

She stepped into the room. Jackson's head was thrown to one side, exposing the frantic beating of his neck. His temples were pulsing. The muscles of his face twitched crazily. His lips were black. His skin was a color she had never seen before, more than the color of sickness, as if overnight Jackson had been varnished with a new color, more intense and more devastating than the color he had taken on weeks ago. His hair was plastered wet to his scalp, curling in ringlets around his ears and neck. Steam rose from him. The bedroom was startlingly cold. She watched the hollow just below his Adam's apple rise and fall like a big purple bruise.

He did not move when she settled on the bed. She stirred the molasses through the water.

"Jackson," she whispered.

His head seemed too large for his body, too large and swollen for him to lift or even turn. She cast about for another pillow. There was one on the rocker. She propped him up. She ladled some water onto the spoon, blowing on it, and dribbled the tiniest bit over his black lips.

"I'm here," she said.

Jackson swallowed. The cords of his neck jerked. Hannah sucked in her breath and looked away.

His hand moved on the quilt. She forced herself to look back at him, to watch his face, to watch his blue eyelids fold open, to watch his brown eyes stare, bewildered, struggling to focus. She forced herself to bring her bandanna from her back pocket and to dab, ever so gently, at each of his temples. She gave him another spoonful of water, but he could not swallow it. It ran out the side of his mouth and down his neck.

"I'm sorry," she said.

Jackson's tongue came out, stark white, and licked his lips.

"I'm sick now," he whispered.

"Yes." She touched him gingerly. She touched just her fingertips to his sunken cheek and felt the muscles jumping below.

"I want to get the doctor to come now," she said.

"No," he said. "Stay with me."

She glanced nervously around the room. She wanted Frisco. No, she wanted Richard, bending over Jackson, smelling of aftershave, taking charge, knowing what to do, calling someone who would wrap Jackson in crisp white sheets and put a breathing mask over his gaping black mouth; she wanted Richard's expensive car parked outside the house, she wanted his leather shoes with the crepe soles padding efficiently across the floorboards, competent, controlled; she wanted the fine tuned machinery of his arms and legs moving here, pouring tea and closing doors and loading up the stove until the house hummed with heat.

"Don't leave me," he rasped.

"I won't," she said quickly.

She took his hand. She smoothed her palm over his fingertips, over the places worn down and rounded into hard stumps by the strings of his guitar. His nails, sliced faithfully each week with the Barlow knife, were jagged and sharp. His knckles were gray, almost black, and swollen with cold. She winced and drew away. Jackson's hand was already dead.

Hannah walked to the bottom of the bed. It was a large bed, pushed to the wall, sagging with age. He had brought Patience to this bed; they had lain here together; they had loved here; she had been conceived here, toward the end of a winter just like this one. Jackson and Patience had warmed one another here all through that night.

She knew what she had to do. She unlaced her workshoes and, placing them side by side, crawled into the bed.

"Come, Jackson," she whispered. "Let me hold you. I'm going to keep you warm so you can sleep."

She was piling blankets all around her as she spoke. She propped herself against the wall. He made no sound as she lifted him. He was all bones. He was as light as a young child. She nestled his face against her breast, careful to keep him breathing, tilting his head back into the crook of her arm. She gathered the quilts all around him, pulling them up over his wasted frame, supporting his back where the vertebrae poked between his shoulders. His eyes opened part way, not seeing anymore, but blinking from time to time. She stroked his wide forehead, lifting the thick matted hair from his brow.

"We'll sing a little," she said, and her voice shook uncontrollably. "Would you like that? Here, I'll sing to you. Do you remember?"

She touched the bristle on his chin and sang a lullaby from the days when Jackson had sat on her bed, sifting his hand through her damp hair, cooling away fevers with songs and sips of whiskey and finger puppets made of newspaper advertisements.

> Hush a bye, don't you cry
> Go to sleep, little lamb.
> When you wake, you shall have
> All the pretty horses.

She sang easy and low; Jackson wheezed and rattled; she began to rock him; she began to lull herself into the rhythm of his dying. In her mind she saw him trudging up from the river on a muggy August morning, swinging a cage full of crabs, smiling; she saw Jackson diving off the rotting piles of the abandoned boat yard, his lean brown arms stroking the dirty water, going out too far, stopping to tread water, throwing back his head and the beads of water flinging like diamonds in the sun; she could see him lying on the rocks, brown as an Indian, the tight muscles of his stomach rising and falling, baking, all summer long, while she built villages in the hard grainy sand, watching the tide come and snatch them away. Jackson's fingertips, at the small of her back, floating her— she remembered them. It was not anything he said that made her know he was aching inside; it was just what children know.

"Jackson?"

She tried to lift his face, but his head was heavy as a stone.

"Can you hear me? Do you know I'm here?"

He swallowed suddenly. It was an awful sound. His body convulsed, pushing both of them into the wall.

She held him tighter. He was suffocating. His eyes flapped open. They were blind, filmed over. She looked away. She began to sing again, louder, and then softer, and then in a whisper. She sang to keep from thinking, to keep from wondering what was going on in Jackson's mind. Was he having thoughts, or was his brain already dead; did he know he was being held, did he know she was there, did he know that this was the last moment, the last thought, the last feeling? Would he feel it if she kissed him, just once, did it matter, did a moment that was never going to be remembered matter? She was barely singing now, she was humming, she had lost track of the tune long ago, she was closing his eyelids with her finger, tracing the line under his brow, she was leaning down, kissing the bridge of his nose, kissing each eye, kissing his forehead, she was drawing her lips along his face, pressing them into the hollow behind his ear, her lips parting, her tongue coming to lick silently at the fine hairs of his neck, of his temples, her hand was running through his hair, her lips were wanting his mouth, she moved to touch it but drew back. His mouth was rotted away. His mouth was black. His mouth was cold and hard and void of any sound. He was dead.

Chapter Two
Patience

Patience

A woman was sitting alone at the counter in a coffee shop in New York. Everything around her moved, but this woman was still as stone. Her hands, resting on the formica, were the deep brown-blond of varnished wood, shot through with veins. Her face had the telltale olive color of a Mediterranean, the dark eyes set under a thick mannish brow, the face wide and flat, the nose big. The whole of it was sturdy, almost ugly, yet in this moment the skin gave forth a light that softened the rough features, and the lips, which could have been hard, were rosy. She was forty-six years old, yet looked easily older. Her hair had gone gray, and there were many lines.

This was Patience.

What she was thinking was critical. As she thought it she felt an initial blindness come over her, not unlike the blindness of a grub that has been overturned by a rake in the garden: weak, exposed, unequipped for light. As she stared into her cold coffee Patience knew suddenly that she had been overturned, that she must head, even blindly, in a new direction. It had been twenty years since she had considered that this direction might be upriver.

For a moment, if anyone had stopped to care, they might have seen astonishment spreading smooth the lines of her face. They might have seen Patience grow young. They would have dismissed the cracked and broken heels, the too dark stockings, the ratted, stinking, fake raccoon, the bruise on the side of one temple. Her face, as if it had been preparing for this moment, was not painted. Her wrists were free of the plastic bangles she always wore. She was now like a statue in the middle of a busy coffee shop, as if a madonna had suddenly cropped up in a hidden garden, a garden hidden in a thoroughfare, spreading her strong hands. She realized all at once that something was about to happen to her, that she had given the inner permission, and that from now on she was going to follow this thing.

Patience took a deep breath.

"Jackson," she whispered.

The oldest memory I have is of my brother Octavio. He is pulling me by the wrist down the school corridor. He holds too tight, and I want to cry out, but I am scared. He brings me as far as the classroom doorway, then he leans down and whispers, "Remember, you are not Patienza anymore, you are Patience." He pushes me from behind and disappears. I feel myself go numb.

I remember a terrible tinkling sound. Later I learned that this was piano music, but when I first heard it I thought that they were all laughing, the blank faces; I thought they were wild with laughter.

I remember the crush of my petticoats against my thighs, and the heavy dress, all handstitched by Honor. I remember the oxblood shoes and the kneecaps, my kneecaps, scrubbed raw as carrots. Scrubbed by Honor, my old grandmother, while my mother watched and smoked.

Perhaps it could be true that I never longed more for Octavio than I did in that moment. For his skin against my skin, for his hand clenching my wrist.

I could not move.

I could not speak.

I could not bring into focus any face.

I thought only of his hand on my wrist. Only of the way my own hand felt light and limp and free, like that of a rag doll caught in the fierce strong grip of a dog. I thought only of Octavio as I stood before them all, feeling the slow sad trickle of urine find its way down my thigh; I thought only of the way his thumb had pressed so violently into the big bone of my wrist.

From that day on I am Patience, though I struggle, all my life, to be Octavio. Sometimes, when I see him from across the lunch tables, or from the top of the sliding board, I feel myself go right out of my body. It is as if I am a boy Octavio's size. It is as if I am Octavio's twin, as if I can be him and be with him all at once.

44   The Red Shirt

This goes on for many years. When I think of childhood I think almost exclusively of Octavio, though in fact I had a mother, and a father, and an old grandmother. I have a rather fantastic memory of them, as if all my childhood were wrapped into a single afternoon, though I know this is a lie. I know this is not true.

This is my memory:
    Upstairs my brother is being beaten. On the ceiling above me pipes and rafters shake. There is the heavy thud of footsteps, of furniture, of Octavio's body being thrown down on the floor. He does not cry out. I am proud of him for not crying out. My undershirt clings to my damp skin. The plastic scapular of the Blessed Virgin sticks in a hollow between my flat bosom, the pale blue ribbon twisting around my sweaty neck. Like an animal I crawl, cowering, back behind the cartons, under the massive pool table, down, down, behind the furnace; I crouch down behind the hot water heater, sweating, itching, trembling with fear. Still he does not cry out. A bottle smashes. A string of rosary beads, left by Honor, hangs from a nail behind the furnace. Help my brother! If you have no beads, Honor has said, count the rosary on your fingers.

Suddenly it is quiet. Too quiet. So very quiet that I cover my ears. Don't let me hear death, I pray. I can hear my heartbeat. It is inside my head, pacing like a

caged animal: right temple, left temple, right temple, left temple.

My brother is building a leaf house. He stands in the forest, ankle deep in leaves. The sun bends over his blond head and his sweaty brown back. He wears a scapular of St. Joseph, tied up with brown ribbon, and he has made his First Communion. He twists the saplings to form a dome, tying them down with rough hemp. He stuffs the frame with leaves. He builds an igloo of leaves, with a poke hole for light, and he smokes inside. Lucky Strike! He passes a cigarette to me. The tip is moist from his lips. Suck on it, he says. I suck. I cough. We sit cross-legged, like Indians, smoking the peace pipe.

We have been thrown off the school bus for being filthy mouthed.

Our father comes at four. His heavy workshoes are caked with mud. They clatter over the flagstones, falling in a heap. I can see them now, the toes curled up with mud, the tops creased and falling over, the rawhide laces stiff with grease, straining upward like pipe cleaners. At four-fifteen our mother pours his demitasse. By four thirty he is asleep, sprawled on the floor in his workclothes. Our mother lights a cigarette. She feeds us food out of cans, her silent nervous *hands fluttering over some cold mess of sauce and noodles. The air is fragile. Swallowing is difficult.*

The white Communion dress is in a box upstairs. We bought it in the department store in town, me and my mother, my mother standing listlessly over the racks of white dresses, her cigarette ash growing long. We bought a square of white linen to make the veil, and the little white gloves, and we bought new white socks with lace cuffs and a white cardboard purse to carry the missal in. It is all upstairs in the old hope chest.

I pull one finger out of one ear. A spider is inching its way down alongside of the rosary. It is black and hairy. I pull the other finger out of the other ear. There is no sound.

In the forest stands the leaf house. The sun is slanting now, bending toward evening. A rabbit hops across the clearing.

Someone is walking across the floor now. The cellar door swings back. A light switches on over the stairs. My mother calls. I don't know where she is, my mother says. She's not in the cellar. The light switches off. The door closes.

Under the cellar stairs are plastic reindeer. There is a wooden manger, no bigger than a shoebox, with a baby Jesus doll, and there are some candles and a Flexible Flyer sled.

There is an angel costume.

Like an animal I slither, silent, from my hiding place. I sniff the air. It is dark, dusty, quiet. Someone walks in the kitchen above. There is the smell of burning coffee. The angel costume hangs on a coat hanger from a nail under the stairs. I must stand on some cartons to reach it. I take the white robe, cut out of a foul smelling sheet, and I take the plastic bag that holds the headdress. The cellar door squeaks. I must open it very carefully.

In the forest I put on the angel robe. I tie the yellow sash. The halo is hard. It is made of coathanger wire, dripping with torn tin foil, and it will not bend right. It digs into my forehead, pinching my temples.

I am an angel!

A single strand of smoke curls from the poke hole of the leaf house. I squat in the doorway. He is in there. His eye is black already. I am careful of my halo as I *come in. He has not cried. His lip is bleeding. He passes me the cigarette.*

The adults were only shadows in the great drama of Octavio and me. In my early memories they are nothing but backdrop.

It was understood between my brother and me, always, that Octavio was first to go into the bush, and that I was to follow, blindly, and so make Octavio hero. My job was that of disciple, and I was happy at it, for I believed, all through our childhood, that Octavio knew what to do. It was not until many years after that I came to see that Octavio and I were like two blindfolded children in a vast labyrinth, slowly weaving our way through a childhood without rules, without words, without response, and, though I fear to say it—without love.

We developed in two distinct ways. Octavio grew to be a brute, a rough defiant boy who was constantly in trouble. He was foul-mouthed, a torturer of animals and small boys, he was a rock thrower, he would spend days deep in the woods devising traps and weapons. His childhood was one full of scrapes and reprimands, he was a delinquent; his initials were painted in every prominent place in the county, and his spot in detention hall was well marked. He ate huge quantities of black licorice and pared his nails with a jackknife. He wore a gold medal of St. Joseph.

I never acquired Octavio's knack for trouble. Not

when I was young. Though I followed my brother and longed to be as defiant, I was, in fact, almost invisible. I rarely spoke when I was a girl, and when I did I stuttered horribly. While Octavio traveled in a pack, I traveled alone, desperately alone, so desperately that when I was not with Octavio I consoled myself only by pretending that I was Octavio.

For many years it went on this way.

Our mother became pregnant in the same year that Octavio was sent to military school. He continued to live at home, but in that year Octavio became a complete stranger to me, and, I suspect, to himself as well. His long blond curls were shorn. His clothes were put away. He wore a severe outfit of blue wool, and he was given a wooden gun. He was forced to take a class in ballroom dancing with some girls from across the river, and during that time he began to say yes sir and yes ma'am. He ceased cursing. Meanwhile our mother swelled and smoked, our father slept, and I wandered forlorn on the school playground, prey to cliques of social butterflies and former victims of my brother's torture. I was alone, without focus, left to trace my brother's name in the dust beneath the swings.

Octavio's career as a soldier was short-lived. After the baby was born he was dismissed from military school (why, I never knew) and my parents had no recourse but to send him back to public school, where he began his sophomore year and I went to the junior high next door. The baby was named Ramona, and with her arrival both my mother and Honor seemed to come briefly to life. I remember coming home from school and being brought into my parents' bedroom, a place dark with mahogany and drawn shades, and there, in a bassinet pinned with gold pieces and holy cards, lay Ramona, a perfect newborn with Octavio's same blond curls. I remember the pride with which my mother untied the sleeves of her little gown, pulling out the tiny fist and slowly uncurling the fingers, one at a time: uno, due, tre. . . . She was perfect. I, on the other hand, was not. Something horrible had begun to happen to me. My brown hair became slick with grease and my face had come to have an oily, filthy sheen. My chin and nose had erupted, my armpits began to stink, but, far worse than any of these things, my undershirt had become too small. To me it meant only one thing—an ending to life as it was, a sudden difference that drew itself down like a curtain between Octavio and me.

Octavio went from boy to man all at once. At seventeen he had left school and married, at eighteen he was a father. I danced at his wedding, all feet. There was a single moment when Octavio broke across the dance floor and swept me into his arms, waltzing me once around the room. I felt the power of his biceps and the strength of his thighs, and then he was gone, forever I thought. I watched the back of him stride away to the bar and my arms hung suddenly empty. That evening I helped tie cans and streamers to the fender of his car and the rattle that they made in the night was a forlorn, woebegone kind of sound.

Octavio had gone into manhood, and that was precisely the place I could not follow him. In the weeks after his marriage my loneliness and despair became acute. I grew to hate my body, for it had betrayed me. It had cut me off, absolutely, from my brother. I felt tricked, as if I had fallen into one of Octavio's homemade traps; it seemed as if every boy who saw me would burst out laughing, seeing the folly I had made, seeing the moment when the pie hit my face. I felt a shame that seared my mind and my body as well. I began to slouch and shuffle. I began to draw my shoulders forward in an attempt to hide those breasts, which to me were the ultimate betrayal; I would gladly have parted with them for just one chance to be able to fool everyone, for I knew in those days that even if I could not follow my brother into manhood, I did not in turn have to accept womanhood. I refused. I shunned womanhood with every ounce of my strength.

Where was my mother during this time? She was doggedly tagging after Ramona, who had begun to toddle and demand, who grabbed for everything and ate everything—Ramona—a thoroughly feminine creature who already was more of a woman than my mother or I would ever be. And as for Honor, she was no help, in her black gunny sack, with her garlic cloves and her mumbo jumbo, with her whiskers and her fondness for anisette.

In all this time my father seems never to have seen me.

52 The Red Shirt

It feels now like I was lost for a very long time, but I know clearly that it was only a year, my sophomore year of high school, and a long distraught summer. It seemed to be the year when my identity as a loner was fused and sealed for good, and something in me gave out, stopped trying to fit, slid into aloneness like a hand into a glove, so that by the time I started my junior year I had no hopes of anything other than being left totally alone.

And so I turned, for the first time, to books. Until that year my schoolwork had never been remarkable. Like Octavio, I had managed to pass most subjects without trouble, occasionally failing a course, rarely excelling. No mention was ever made of schoolwork at home. I suspect that my parents saw school only as a way station, a place to store children until they were big and strong enough for real work. I often think this attitude may have been most helpful in my discovery of books, for never once in my life had I experienced the pressure that other children have borne and buckled beneath. The books were completely my own endeavor.

And so, without realizing what I had stumbled upon, I casually entered a way of life that was to become mine from that year on—the intellectual life. For this I was tortured. It happened because I could not contain myself. In English class my arm seemed to shoot up as if entirely of its own accord. There was forever a question or comment on my lips. I challenged everything. I wrote essays when none were required. I wrote in the margins of schoolbooks and I wore down the resources of Miss Ames, the librarian. Meanwhile a firecracker went off in my locker, my purse was flushed down a toilet in the boys' john, the elastic was let out of my gymsuit, and once, while standing to make a point in history class, my shoelace was tied to the leg of my chair, causing me to drag it almost halfway across the room.

Did it matter? I wonder now. I wonder what kind of damage it did. I would watch boys stroll by in their tight groups, longingly, and I remember thinking that it must have been some kind of mistake, my being a girl—my being a smart girl at that.

My brother's wife was hard of hearing. Because of this she seemed always far away, in a dreamworld, for the moment she looked away she lost track of conversations, and sometimes she muttered under her breath, as if not realizing that others could hear. She was young. Like Octavio, she had quit school. She was intent on having a family, on keeping a house, on setting a good table and sewing a straight seam. She was a hard worker, never complaining, though to me she often seemed dull, almost dim witted.

But she was beautiful. I feared her for this reason. Her beauty was uncommon. It was arresting. I always supposed that it was partly due to her deafness that she held herself so strongly, as if ever alert, and this had served her well, for her back and shoulders were strong and straight, her very shoulder blades were beautiful, and her strong, sure arms were sturdy and lean. She was lean all over, her belly flat and tight, her jaw was large and extraordinarily well defined. Her brow was high and smooth, paring back into lovely temples; her eyes were of a thick blond honey color and her hair was as rich and rosy as chestnuts. She was most wonderfully graceful and expressive, especially in her arms and hands, and she was gay; she had a laugh that chortled into the air like water from a jug. This was for me a paradox, how a woman could exude such intelligence and yet never have an intelligible thing to say. I always felt that there was some secret in her.

Octavio loved her in a practical and passionate way. He needed her. He had entered into marriage with her barely knowing her name, and for him this was the mystery and the beauty of love, to wake beside a stranger who was as young and handsome as himself, and so to love without thinking, day by day, until the bond was set. For a long time, whenever she came into a room he would start, as if meeting her for the first time, and he was extremely courteous to her, as if she were one of the girls he had danced with back in military school under the watchful eyes of a captain. He was stiff and formal, yet, always, his eyes were full of moon when they lighted on her.

As I said, I was afraid of her. Though I did not know it at the time, it was her rage that I most feared, as if some instinct was at work in me, as if I knew that a woman's rage could be fiercer than any man's tirade. I believed that she was better than me, for she had won the prize and I was left standing behind the gate, and like a robber, I feared that one day I would make that gate creak, and be caught reaching for the prize. In time I did make it creak, and my life has never been the same. It was Octavio who finally gave me my own femininity. To this day I fear the rage of his woman.

It happened in autumn. I had begun college, much against my parents' wishes. I was hopelessly overwhelmed owing to the fact that I had done so poorly in high school. I struggled to catch up, but my vocabulary was no more than a laundry list, and, despite my love of books, I had hardly read enough of them to be considered properly read. I was failing.

My brother had purchased an orchard out in the countryside. It contained a wild grape arbor swollen with purple fruit, and a twisted row of trees: quince, apples, pears and peaches. It was not a large piece of land, barely an acre, but for Octavio I knew it was a link to the woods of his childhood, a place to sit and dream and smell and tend. I remember how the branches hung low and pregnant that day when I came down through the tall grass, carrying my books, starting in surprise as I almost tripped over him.

"But 'Tavio!" I cried, "Why are you out here in the middle of the day?"

My brother was lying in the weeds, smoking.

He was drunk.

"I'll quit that stupid job yet," he said slowly. "I work hard, but I ain't nobody's mule."

I remember standing there above him. It must have been a full minute before I realized that this was the first time I'd been alone in the woods with my brother since we were children. There was an excitement to it, something that made my arms crawl with gooseflesh.

The woods around us lay silent and bloated with heat. The branches of the overgrown trees strained to hold the heavy fruit. I remember that I felt nauseous, the way nausea is always present in joy. The sight of my brother lying back in the grass was so terribly beautiful, so perfectly familiar, so innocent, so delicate. He was like a boy, lean and innocent and generous, like a prince, like a dream. I remember how my heart raced.

Octavio reached up to one of the branches and twisted off an apple.

"Taste it," he said.

I remember that there was never an apple so sweet. I ate it hungrily, hunching down beside him, laying my books on the ground.

When I threw away the apple core, I began to cry. I cried for a long time. Octavio smoked. He looked off into the distance. His face was grave and sad.

"Hey," he whispered. "What is this?"

"I can't do it," I sobbed. "I can't do it, 'Tavio. I'm failing. I try so hard, but there's so much reading, and then come the papers, and the lectures, oh God, where I can barely understand what they mean, and everyone else is so smart—"

"Hey, hey," he clucked. His face became red. "You think those pussies are smarter than you? None of them would last ten minutes on a work crew! You're smarter than all of them put together!"

He was fierce and sincere. His brow was wet with passion.

"You'll show them all!" he cried, making a fist.

I had stopped crying, like a child who has been distracted by some bright object. I stared at him.

"But I have no friends!" I blurted.

We were embarrassed suddenly. Octavio looked away.

"You need a boyfriend," he said softly.

What I remember then is that my hand went to my throat, and that I almost cried out. In a single instant I felt enraged, disgusted, ashamed and sad.

"But I'm so ugly," I said.

Octavio spun around.

"Ugly?" His mouth dropped in surprise. "You think you're ugly?" he asked.

His hand groped for the cigarettes in his T-shirt sleeve. His fingers shook.

I could feel a single tear run down my face, hot in the sun. The air was seared with the sound of locusts. I could feel the dull ache of hatred for my body—I could feel the hatred swell—I wanted to turn and butt my head into the trunk of the apple tree—I wanted to butt it until I was blind. I began to cry again, this time in big halting sobs. Then I felt the weight of my brother's hand as he laid it on my shoulder.

"All my life I've wanted to be you!" I cried.

I had sunk to my knees in the grass.

Octavio knelt beside me. He took my face into his hands and held me close to him.

I froze. I kept still while I felt his thumb begin to nudge my face. I felt excited to my core, as if part of me were reeling at the speed of light, and part of me was stopped like a photograph from long ago, frozen, ages old, startled by a sudden great flash. Passion, which had never touched me before, now swelled like an instant bruise—tender, full of pain, full of reaction—I came so fully to life that I felt as if I'd been struck, over and over, and was only now beginning to realize it, and, for a second, almost loved it, as if being struck was as exhilarating as it was painful, for it was life, it was a real feeling, it was a stirring up of matter that had become solid and almost dead. I felt my brother's thumb grab hold of my nipple, and once again, as I had done so symbolically all my life, I threw back my head and bared my throat to his hungry lips, and I felt him take my vein in his mouth, sucking it, and then we were down in the dust and the grass, down in the earth that was thick with the smell of fermenting apples, rolling, tumbling, his flesh into my flesh, his arms my arms, his wrists my wrists, his smell familiar, as if I had touched him all my life, as if his temples were my temples, as if his lips were mine, as if I could be with him and be him all at once, my Octavio, my darling, my heart.

 He rose above me then, and as he worked me his eyes watched mine.

 "Have lots of men," he said, panting, "because you are beautiful."

 And then he cried out, rolling up his eyes. In the tree above us a bird called. I held my brother to me and was afraid.

 What happened had happened so fast. We did not linger the way lovers lingered. We had torn at one another like famished animals, and afterward we gathered ourselves up hastily, our eyes slanting sideways. We could not talk. We dared not touch again. Octavio was first to leave. He turned only once, just before he left the orchard; his face was grim and confused; he looked at me for a long time, and then he raised his hand, just for a moment, and I did not see him again for many years.

I quit school. It seemed useless to go on. I wanted only to be anonymous, to be lost in a great sea of people, of men in particular, for, having tasted my brother I knew that I was doomed, all my life, to find a man like him. My brother had made me feel beautiful where I had felt ugly; his single act had made me bold; his dominance had at last been fulfilled in my body, and I lived only to repeat it. I wanted nothing more than to be dominated over and over again.

I went to New York. It was the only place I knew on earth that was vast enough, filled with hungry men into whose eyes I could gaze and search and pretend. I did not mind the whoring—the whoring made me feel tight and high and beautiful. The whoring taught me to weave my hips when I walked; it raised my chin and made me strong—it made me, strangely—it made me feel like a strong young boy, as if I had balls, as if I were hard and muscled and in control—the whoring made me set my jaw against the gritty New York mornings as if I were a bold young man of war. Like my brother before me, I became the brute, the deviser of traps, the teaser of small boys. Soon I was well known.

The Red Shirt

Strange new people began coming to town. They were reading poetry and tuning guitars, and I had barely discovered them when I met Jackson Spencer.

I had been in the city just over a year, turning tricks, and had not yet met a man like Octavio. When I was not working I spent time in the coffeehouses and bookshops. The folksingers were coming out bit by bit and I went to hear them, to see if someone like my brother might be there, for the folksingers seemed rough and soft, all at once, as if they knew some of the things that my brother had known.

On the night I heard Jackson he made little impression on me. I stayed in the bar only because it was warm and the whiskey was flowing. I stayed until lights out. I got drunk. I stumbled out into the street and he came running after me with his big guitar case, and I thought he would be easy money, a wimp, a beatnik, and so I brought him to my room where he sat on the edge of the bed and stared at me, and then I saw what I had been looking for—the sturdy rough hands, the tender shadowy temples, the broken teeth and the heavy workshoes and the veined forearms and the red flannel shirt—the quivering, bitter mouth, the beaten eyes. He did not fuck me that first night. He did not touch me at all. I did not know why he was there. Though I had power that I could have worn like a scent, I knew that I was neither physically beautiful nor striking. I was a street whore—hard, lean, young, full of hate. To have a man sit on the edge of my bed and consider me was something like an interruption or an annoyance.

"What do you want?" I asked him. My hand was already fumbling for my garter.

"Nothing," he said. "I only want to look at you."

"Why?"

"I don't know," he answered. "I feel as if you belong somewhere else. You are unnatural here. When I saw you in the bar I only knew that it was wrong, that you are masquerading, that you are just a girl in dress-up and that you need to get out of here. Come on up the river," he pleaded. "Your life will change."

He came to me every week, and when I lay with him I smelled earth and grass and water. His body was spare and restless, like that of a boy, and his kisses were frantic and hungry. He put me in mind of what I had lost: his threadbare jeans, his scrawniness, his masculinity that was at the same time delicate, like the fragile pulse of fine china when it is held to the lips. I began to feed off him. I began to feel my own bones. I became a boy again, deep in the woods; I became Jackson's comrade, Jackson's disciple. His tenderness brought me out of my body, for he demanded no feminine games, no lies, he sought to extract nothing from me, in fact he loved my hardness, he loved my boyness, and so when things got rough, when whoring turned sour, I went away from the city and moved up the river with him.

I never learned much about Jackson's life before me. He kept pretty quiet about it. He had been raised by his mother up in New England somewhere, Vermont, maybe New Hampshire. She worked hard, and he didn't see much of her. He'd caught on to the music early in his life, square dances and contra dances, up in Brattleboro and Concord. It took hold of him the way religion takes hold of some, like a bloodsucker. I don't know where or how he learned, I only know that he did, and I like to imagine my Jackson as a teenager, all bones, tuning up that old Martin with an ear that was born to it.

I was not in love with him. To this day I am unable to fall in love, unable to give up the dream of Octavio. To this day I refuse my womanhood—I hide it, I spit on it, I strangle its every sound. But in that brief time with Jackson, when I was a boy beside him, I was happy. I loved the woods and the river and the trashy little town. I loved the strength of my lover's arms as if they were my own arms, and I envied his sex, and I pretended, almost successfully, that I was him, that his jutting hips were my hips, that his scratchy beard was mine. For a year I played this game. We lived in great peace. He worked in the factory and I spent my days roaming the woods and reading, always reading, and we spoke little and made love much, and I saw Jackson fall deeply in love with me, and when that happened I saw him begin to panic, for both of us knew that I had not fallen, that I could never fall, that I was incapable of falling.

Jackson devised ways to hold me. The child was completely his idea, and he talked incessantly about nothing else. He stopped drinking. He came home from his singing sober and sad, and pleaded and cried and held me to him as if I were a balloon full of helium.

"Don't leave me."

He said it day and night.

I had no notion of leaving. I was happy being a boy in the woods. Sometimes I would think of seeing my brother again, but I was afraid. My love for him had only magnified.

I became pregnant. I knew right away that Jackson had trapped me, had pricked a hole in the safe, had lied and schemed in his fear of losing me.

"You'll see," he said. "It will make all the difference. I'll become famous, you'll see, and then you will be glad you stayed."

Jackson worked at becoming famous all through my pregnancy. He sang until he was hoarse and no one heard him.

In pregnancy, my body began to do something utterly feminine and utterly out of my control, and as I grew fat and soft I could feel the boy I loved begin to claw at the walls of me, and I will say that what I experienced during those months was true craziness, for I no longer knew who I was or what I thought; I knew only the panic of this boy, this precious boy that I had fought all my life to preserve, and as he weakened and shriveled and began to die I felt myself begin to die; I felt lights going out all through myself, one by one; it was excruciating, it was devastating, so that by the time that baby came out of me I was completely wrecked, completely forsaken, completely out of my mind.

What can I say about the baby? I did not love her. Yet she was so exquisite! Her little hands, her feet, the down of her hair, all were exquisite. She was so full of life. Her cry was lusty and ferocious, her eyes were round with intelligence. She was helpless in a way that moved me deeply, but I could not love her. I was out of my mind. I saw the baby from a great distance, as if through a tunnel, or a kaleidoscope, and when Jackson held her and loved her with all his heart I felt only a frozenness, a disability, and a desire to run.

He wanted me to love her. He was desperate for me to love her. Sometimes he would take my hand in his and lay it over her little body, as if coaxing warmth, as if somehow their flesh together could stimulate mine.

I did not want to see her grow up. Something terrified me about the fact that she would one day speak and think and form an opinion of me. That she would confront me with my inadequacy. That she would hate me.

I fled. I was reabsorbed into the city overnight.

There seems little to say about my life after that. I am, after all, nothing but an old whore, rather useless now, rather lonely. Though my body has been satisfied, my heart continues to bleed, so much that sometimes it is all that I can bear to stay alive, and I wonder why I do it—I wonder why I continue to breathe and eat and sleep when it is so pointless and I am so tired.

I saw Octavio once more, though he did not see me. It was such a terrible miracle, almost a science fiction, to round a corner in Times Square and see him, his hand cupped into the nape of a young child's neck, his face raw and bland and happy, his wife leaning into the crook of his arm—it was Christmastime—there was a jingling of bells—I fell back in a doorway and let my brother pass.

In the coffee shop Patience was rising to leave. She seemed in a hurry now. She pushed her way out into the cold February street. She carried a large black vinyl pocketbook. She folded her matted collar up over the tender spot on her face. She shrugged.
    Sometimes you get hurt.
    She stopped, lit several matches before she could get a cigarette going. Her worn heels clacked on the icy sidewalk. She headed for Grand Central.

In my memory of Octavio's wedding my mother is standing in the dirt and gravel driveway of our home

outside Liberty. She is dressed in evening clothes, the silk of her gown is colorless in the moonlight. She has slipped out of her high heels and they stand sentinel beside her like two little dogs. Over her evening dress my mother wears Octavio's black leather jacket. The thing fits her like a huge piece of armor, for it has long ago molded to his body. My mother smokes, and her hair tucks into the collar of Octavio's jacket and knots of it keep escaping into the breeze. They keep escaping and blowing up into the breeze, evaporating. Beside the shoes my mother's ankles and feet are sagging. Where are the fine creases, the chipped stones of her ankles, where are the tight hard calves—where? What happened? What happens to young women when they see this thing, this collapse, this first hint that mother is not beautiful, not ravishing, not called away from her children because of her exquisiteness, but rather for some other reason, some worse reason, some reason they do not ever want to entertain?

She is trying to joke with Octavio's friends. She gets a light. Her laughter in the night is on the verge of panic.

I am in the MG. It is hidden halfway in the woods, rusted, rotting, abandoned by Octavio and his new wife. I have rolled up the windows and I sit low, in the vines and mouse pellets, watching my mother get drunk with boys.

I sit in a cloud of organdy. My dress fills all my lap.

The train was a local. Patience sat very still. She tried to keep her back very straight. She tried to imagine his face, now, but it was not Jackson who kept coming to her. It was, rather, the baby, except that she was a different baby. The baby Patience saw was Ramona, lying in a bassinet pinned with gold pieces and holy cards, and, as she watched her, Patience thought she could once again feel the boy, her boy, the one who had nearly died, the one who had fled, and it all became a jumble in her mind: the baby, Octavio, Jackson, Ramona, until Patience, dizzy and overheated, pressed her forehead to the window and slept.

There was a path coming up from the river to the house. It was only a few inches wide, coming up through reeds and cattails and it smelled rank and the earth was clay, beaten down and slimy, and it would slap and spring back under their feet when they ran up from the river because of the urgency. The urgency with which he would fling back the door and hunt for the whiskey while Patience pulled one arm out of his sweaty T-shirt and ran her hands over the silky red mosaic of his tatoo; they were always in a hurry, tripping across the train tracks, skidding around the dirt at the corner of the house.

Sometimes they would stay right there in the weeds, right where they had been reading or talking or smoking. Patience would crawl down on all fours where the water lapped up in her face, salty and dense, and Jackson would put it to her from behind, his face staring with surprise out over the water, just for a moment, before he buried his nose in the skin between her shoulder blades where he could smell her oil and feel the vibration of her backbone.

Chapter Three
The Closet

The Closet

His yellow curls would not behave on the day of the funeral. For some reason Frisco had thought the rubber band improper, and so he had brushed the hair out into its full glory of ringlets, and there it fell, chest length, whipping uncontrollably in the bleak February wind, so that he saw only snatches of her, so that Hannah stood as if on the other side of a golden curtain, apart from him, and he had to keep snatching back the veil to see when she cried, when she gave way—but she never did. She just stood in the ice cold blast wearing only overalls and her father's red flannel shirt. Her shoulders were straight as sawhorses, and her eyes, from what he could tell, were dry.

This worried him. He did not know much about grieving, though his life had been so full of sorrow that he knew enough to recognize damage, his own damage, and so now it was his own lack of tears, once again, that led him to know, instinctively, that Hannah's frozen body, standing on the grave, was nothing more than a can of worms, that can of worms that gets us all, he thought; the one that will someday burst on her, oozing worms that will never stop moving and eating and repulsing and confusing her—he stopped here—the thought of Jackson's rotting body interjected itself, and Frisco looked down, glad suddenly for his tangle of hair.

I've never been very strong, he thought, ashamed, putting his hands into his pockets.

As he had loved the father, so now he loved Jackson's daughter, obsessively, uncontrollably, in a way that made him miserable and nauseous. She was, to Frisco, painfully beautiful, a study in flat planes and strong, steady curves. Her round sallow moonface, bereft of its summer brown, was like the deep inner flesh of a burst, sun ripened pit, *passion fruit,* he thought, *breadfruit,* some dense meaty fruit that a man could suck and devour and turn over between his palms.

A man. A man could do that, but not a boy.

She was as unreachable as the moon and stars, there, being led away from the grave in the long protective herringboned arms of Richard O'Connor. She was the maiden at the prow of a ship, wooden and unmoved in great turbulence, her shoulders like a rod of steel beneath Richard's professional hands— his button pushing hands, his controlling hands, his finger raised for silence in the little yellow kitchen, his hands gently prying the shot glass from Jackson's grasp.

Richard.

Frisco felt himself go down. He felt the snow melt instantly on his patched and faded kneecaps. Very quietly he allowed his forehead to rest in the ice.

"I'll take care of her, Jackson," he whispered. "If she'll let me, I will."

Good-bye.

It was such a hideous word.

Such a dull, deaf, dead, final word.

Such a gradual word. Like the slow, long, aching, everlasting rising of the sun, like the ache of realization, the dawning of consciousness, the robber bird circling once, twice, three times over the cliffs of knowing. Knowing all that long winter that February would bring good-bye. Would bring a mound of frozen dirt and a cluster of shy factory workers. Would bring the half empty whiskey flask that slid so easily from under the seat of the pickup as Frisco ground the old decrepit gears, hard, and pumped the aging, bare-metal gas pedal, clapping his hands harder and harder against the cold. Good-bye.

He kept the clutch pushed in. He sat, clapping his hands in anger now, applauding the way one applauds a bullfighter who leaves the ring bloodied and numb, unable to so much as wave. Oh Jackson.

Frisco clapped on, and his hands grew warm. He let the truck run. Slowly a rhythm came into his head, a memory, a line:

The Red Shirt

> Don't stand close to the candy man,
> He'll ease a stick of candy in your hand.

They had met seven months ago, in a bar, though to Frisco Jackson had been no stranger. He had seen and watched and copied and studied Jackson Spencer all his life, with all the enthusiasm and obsession of a lover, or of a boy in need of a father, or of a disciple in need, bad need, of a master. The Hudson was deep in the heart of summer then, lush, moist, blue with heat and humidity, a great hothouse for passions of all kinds, and the fiddler, yearning for his moment, was no exception. He was no different from boys who stood at the summer windows of girls, lusting, blanketed with the oppression of loneliness, self-hate, jealousy. It was not a lover Frisco was after, it was a legend, a whisper, a rumor on the wind that had teased his ear all his life, since the day he had sat cross-legged on the lunchroom floor at school sniffing the strong scent of disinfectant and hearing the sound of what he now knew to be his beloved's voice: Jackson Spencer, whose own little girl sat nearby, though Frisco would never know it, and did not even know it now.

The bar had been cool, cold in fact, and Jackson had bent painfully over the strings of the old Martin after every song, retuning, patient, reaching for the mason jar, swallowing, retuning. Frisco sat as if on an electric wire, oblivious to the chatter and static around him. He sat at the base of a great mountain, and decided that this, finally, would be the night he would climb. He kept his fiddle box under his chair, his bare toes curled around it like the greedy fingers of a newborn.

When the break came, he approached.

"Mr. Spencer."

Frisco eased himself onto a bar stool, trying to be casual.

Jackson was screaming at a woman who sat at Frisco's elbow. In the long moment it took for him to scream his drunken proposition, Frisco gazed into his heated face and studied the man he had loved so instantly, so long ago. It broke his heart open to be so close, to at last see every pore, the snarl of the roughened lips, the wet oily tumble of hair long unwashed, the green-purple-yellow tinge that alarmed Frisco, that showed him immediately and irrevocably that the man was dying.

"Mr. Spencer, I . . ."

Frisco leaned past the woman, desperate, feeling his skull tremble violently.

". . . I wonder if I could buy you a drink."

So it has always begun with disciples and masters, that first drink. That first meager droplet of an offering that magically becomes an ocean of give and take, of more equality than the two ever admit, but the equality, through instant respect, that is always there.

Jackson leaned forward, his large brown eyes struggling to see beyond the glint of Frisco's spectacles.

"Are you sure you want to?"

"Yes."

"Okay then."

It was four in the morning when they reached the

house. Frisco was in a dream, a dream of twenty years in its making, and the girl was only part of it, only a brief part, only a round spooky face peeping from behind a stamped Indian cloth.

"Doesn't talk," Jackson muttered, drunk, his words as soft and fluid as molasses. Then, louder, "He's hungry, Hannah."

She came, wearing a man's faded flannel wrapper, her large bare feet creaking unsteadily over the boards, her eyes thick-lidded with sleep. Her hair was knotted in a long braid, thick as a man's fist, wiry and brown, streaked with summer reds and yellows, all of it playing in the lamplight as she flitted from stove to sink to her place on the floor before her father, where she began to unlace the leather straps of his shoes. She was so obviously his daughter. Every movement was his. The sharp, bony wrists, the overgrown ankles and feet, the jerk of shoulders, the tight, boyish buttocks. Only the face was different, neither sharp nor tight, but swollen, round as the moon and browner than any white face he had ever seen. The eyes were Jackson's, but the brow was something primitive and wild, smeared like putty and intensely sorrowful.

The interaction of her and Jackson was silent and tender. Once Jackson reached out with unsteady fingers and casually brushed back one of her reddish hairs and the girl glanced away awkwardly, skittish, and then back, up, and Frisco watched her quickly and quietly pat the calf of his leg, as if to tell the drunkenness that it would pass, that morning would soon be there to end it. The kettle roared.

From all of this he hung back, afraid, on tenterhooks,

living the first real night of his life, the first wakeful dream. He stood lost by a stained calico curtain in the open doorway, his fiddlebox gathered to his throbbing heart, until slowly, with the grace of a fisher casting her reel, the girl, who now changed instantly to woman, extended a mug of steaming tea, and Frisco, reaching for it, stepped inside.

"Play a little something," Jackson commanded, sleepily, and as the girl disappeared back behind her curtain, Frisco slowly drew his bow.

Now, in the truck, he watched Richard crossing the graveyard. In a moment he was at the window, propping his hand on the side mirror, leaning in so that Frisco could light him a cigarette. Their eyes met, and for the first time since the death Frisco could feel tears wanting to form, really wanting to, though as unable as ever.

"We didn't make it in time," Richard said softly.

He smoked for a long time, almost the whole cigarette, and then he reached in his breast pocket and pulled out a small cassette tape in a black box, offering it almost apologetically, yet with pride, Frisco saw, and with conviction.

"This is all I got," Richard said.

He reached for another cigarette, thought a moment, and put it back.

"I fly for California tonight," he said. "I'm sorry. I'll drive Hannah home, if you don't mind. I'd like a moment with her. I'd like to tell her what I saw in Jackson, if I can, so she'll know why I cared so much. You know already. You know he was great."

Frisco nodded dimly. Yes. He knew. His fingers burned on the plastic box.

"She needs your care," Richard said.

"I will—" Frisco said immediately.

"I know."

Richard pulled himself up straight, moving as if to touch Frisco, but he did not. He only turned, and it was to the back of him that Frisco said, "Thank you." Richard shrugged, nodded.

"Okay now," he said. "Okay, good-bye."

Frisco rolled off the cap of Jackson's abandoned whiskey flask and let the stuff jug down his throat in a burst of steam. It was a little like crying, the way the whiskey caused his pipes to jerk.

At the house everything was still. The guitar case stood propped in the corner like a small black coffin, like the coffin of a baby, Frisco thought. Something that had cried and cried, but never been allowed to grow. Something had stopped Jackson, and it had been something far bigger than death.

Hannah was nowhere to be found. He thought that she must be up tending to the goats, or perhaps gone off into the woods. He stoked the kitchen stove and began a fire. Two hours passed. It was then that Frisco first realized that she was not gone off, but was there, right inside the house, as if her odor had at last come to him, absolutely silent, still as snow falling deep in the night. She was there. Hannah was somewhere.

With a terrific beating in his heart Frisco threw back the curtain to her room, but she was not on the bed, nor wedged in the space between the wall and the dresser. Yet he knew, with certainty, that she was there with him, as if she had coughed or sneezed, as if she had whimpered.

The closet, he decided at last, going to the doorway of Jackson's room. The closet door was indeed shut, her presence wafting from it like smoke on the air. Frisco stood in his hiking boots on the cold lonely floorboards and gently called her name.

"I never had anyone to love before," Frisco said quietly.

It was late. The ark of day had shifted in its great watery berth; twilight lapped at the stern. Through the damp floorboards Frisco could smell the ice that was forming on the river. He thought quickly of Jackson's body, crushed with the weight of the earth, and he tilted the flask, once, and settled it on the floor beside him. He sat with his shoulder hunched into the closet door, his back cradled in the molding of the corner. With heavy fingers he began to plait a braid in his long yellow hair.

It was one thing, not to have been loved, Frisco thought, bending his wrists over the braid; it was another thing not to have been allowed to love back anyway. Not to have had any responsibility. Not to have grown up burdened with caring, with loyalty, with love, incestuousness, duty, secrets. Emptiness seemed a worse punishment than any of that could ever have been. Who had there been for him? Whose shoes to bend and unlace, whose vomit to mop, whose step to tremble at? None. The temperate climate of television, the hiss of sprinkler systems, the blat-blat of tired tires over the driveway grate, the fantail of wrought iron. Carpet. Carport. Milk bottles. Washcloths draped over foreheads, feet up, stewed tomatoes and prunes. He had never been touched.

On the other side of the door he could feel her swelling, throbbing, engorged with grief.

"I've got whiskey," he whispered. "Whiskey, Hannah."

Still she would not answer. He got up, stumbling, and went into the bathroom, just behind the closet. The walls of the house were thin enough for him to put his fist through. Frisco knew this. He sighed. He switched on the light. In a cracked mirror strung over the toilet bowl he saw himself, one half of his hair braided loosely to his chest, the rest fallen and cascading over the pocket of his workshirt. His eyes were encircled in black, back behind the little glasses, they were pale and drunk and alone.

He let his water go. He heard Hannah listen to it fly, heard her come to attention—how often had she sat in the kitchen and listened to her father piss—how closely they had lived, how tiny and intimate this house was, so that even now, as he stood and relieved himself Frisco could feel the very hairs on the back of her neck, and, as if in confirmation, he heard a small rustling sound in the closet.

"Will you talk to me?" he asked.

There was no answer. Frisco went and tended the fire.

"I've got whiskey," he said, standing over the stove. "It's warm out here in the kitchen."

She was not going to talk. She was back in it, the same silence she had been in when he met her, before she knew for certain that her father was dying, back when she was just a child running from her senior year of high school, a failed graduation, a silent tender of goats, tender of garden, tender of laundry, of red shirts and patched, faded denims, tender of beat up guitars cracking into table edges, tender of hamburger meat and whiskey and tea.

"Please," he said. "Please, Hannah, don't."

But who knew what it had been like, how the hours had gone when they finally found her in the bed clutching his stiff body, her head hung down low to avoid the sudden light, her refusal to meet any eyes, her hands raw and bitter with cold. What had passed between them all that long afternoon before Frisco arrived, whistling his way into the kitchen as on any other night, waiting for Richard, roaring up the stove, wondering what the quiet was, why the house was so cold, knowing, as he knew now, that something had gone silent, again, that a life had been snuffed out. Now hers, there in the closet, was being snuffed out moment by moment—she was dying with something—speech—the thing she had lost and gained again, and now here it was flown off—she was in a ball, he was sure, her face resting in the muddy rawhide laces and uppers of his workshoes, her breasts swathed in the musty worn flannel of his shirt, she was shivering in there, and if he had any sense he would fling back the door and grab her by the shoulders and begin to shake and shake and shake and shake her. . . . She was sick. Psycho. She'd never been right. She'd been screwed from the day he met her. She was off. Flipped out. Lovely.

Frisco stood at the stove and took a long drink. The tips of his fingers, calloused with years of playing, slid easily over the crease of his lips, smearing the liquor. He kissed his thumb, tenderly, as if it were the dense hard lower lip of a woman, a young strong woman, as if it were Hannah's lip, thick and hard and frozen with silence.

"Let me hold you," he called loudly. "For Chrissake, Hannah, come out of there and let me hold you."

Let me warm you, he thought. Let me take care of you, look after you, father you, mother you, lover you, give you some gift that no one has ever accepted from me. Let me care. Let me love. Not the way I loved Jackson. Not the way that sits out on a barge on the river and calls across the water and moves slowly out of sight, hauled away like a dog on a rope following the boss, the tug, the chief.

(I would have lain with Jackson, he thought, quickly, I would have lain with him in a second.)

Not the way you stand behind somebody on a wooden fruit crate and saw a horsehair bow until your muscles scream just so that, somewhere, when you least expect it, he flings his head back in your direction and gives you thirty seconds of air time. Not that way.

This way.

The way I go to the closet door and open it a crack, and let in the smallest of lights, and there you are, crazy and silent and rolled up into a rag doll with your eyes squeezed shut into the tongues of his shoes and I lean in that place, dark with damp and mold, and I take back that thick braid of yours, like a tassel of the finest silk, and I lay my lips, hot from the heat of the kitchen, right into the nape of your neck, I lay them, and I bring my arm around you, and you are not crazy anymore—you are fine—you look up at me and we are okay, and we have a beginning—a beginning of what happened that first time, when I ducked in through the calico curtain of your father's yellow kitchen, when you kept your eyes down but looked at me all the same, I know about it, when damage met damage and I wanted to cry, like I want to cry now, like I want to sit down here at the closet door and cry the crying that you won't cry—Christ, girl, Christ, child, what are you thinking? What are you feeling? How have you gone to stone so suddenly, so finally?

"I'll open it," he said, out loud, rattling the doorknob. "I swear I'll open it if you don't come out."

Chapter Four
Agony

Agony

I am Hannah. It's all that I know. I am Hannah. Somewhere Hannah is, I know it, small and buried, like a secret, like a pineal gland, a little ink spot of control, a little jellied jujube of Hannahness left melting on a great tongue of madness while I lay here with no hands and no feet, everything tied down but my belly, which is folded carefully over inside like a soft wallet, like the kind of wallet a man like Richard would have, folded and full of dirty government notes that have words scrawled on them, words like *committed, insane, tranquilized, muscle relaxed, diapered, out of control.* From the little pea-sized crystal that is Hannah comes a big sound, comes the ripping and shredding of the cords of her neck, comes the thrashing and thrashing and thrashing of muscles next to bones that are locked down, pinned tight in sheepskin, mesh, buckles, people, fear, panic, a terror greater than anything the size of a jujube can sustain, melting, losing track of hands, of feet, of skin and hair, of thought, of Jackson's red shirt, soaked black with sweat underneath all that sheepskin, underneath all that lamby wool and something—something squirted into me that drips now, drip, drip, drip, drip, drip, drip. I am Hannah. I know it; I can smell the grease of his red flannel collar; I can smell the place where his hair met his neck, that hollow of his neck, where the oil of my father's tiny jujube melted into his collar and became the red shirt; I can smell my father as I twist my head from side to side and I am Hannah; nothing can take it away, though it is melting—liver, kidneys, deep purple guts all are leaving me—daddy, oh daddy, oh my daddy come for me now, come take me with you, come get me out of this bright light, out of this clean smell, out of this movement, this blur, this inability to kick, to curl up, to explode, to crack my skull into a thousand splinters that will go with you, that will give you my brains, delivered like hot steaming afterbirth into your hands—oh daddy, oh Jackson, hold my brains now, take my brains—I'm going out, I'm going out of my mind, there are hands all over me, there are voices all around me, there is not one thing that is mine, not one thing but flannel. I live above the table in a bubble the size of a thumbnail, I cleave to a spot on the wall where my blood is. They are holding my head. Many hands are holding my head. I see a long, fine black thread pull out, go back in. It doesn't matter. The candy of me is melted. The candy man. It is a droplet in a bubble on the wall billowing from a spot of my own blood and it sings a little song from across the room:

> Don't stand close to the candy man,
> He'll ease a stick of candy in your hand.

It started as a decision, but now it is beyond decision. Now it is beyond reason. Now I am completely lost. I have been blown up. I have been hit, and blown up, and I am lying here on fire, and Hannah is over there now. I am still. Nothing will move now. Nothing will ever move again. If I keep it all very still, if I manage to move not one cell of it Jackson will stay with me. The collar here, the bubble there. That is all that matters. I promise to be good. I promise not to move.

The tug of silk on my bare scalp. My eyelids. My lungs. Nothing else must move. My eyelids. My lungs. Behind my eyes there is a river of tears, deeper and mightier than the Hudson, black and salty, riddled with history that runs in veiny rivulets down my father's chest. I am Hannah, holding still, dispersing slowly, unaware that I have left my body and gone with dad, over there; we are in a bubble, we are in a dream, nothing can hurt us now, nothing can stop us from what we were meant to have, to do, to be. My dad and me. We were meant to be somewhere else. I always knew that.

"I'm sorry, but I don't seem to have a light. Is this a smoking car? No?"

Patience stretched and stretched.

"Peekskill?" she asked, with a wave of her ticket. "The station is still there, right?"

"Alive and kicking, lady," the conductor answered, punching her stub of cardboard, glancing at the torn black stockings and battered heels.

He moved on.

The Red Shirt

"It's been a while," Patience said to a man across the aisle. He did not glance up from his paper.

What's happened to me, she thought suddenly. What have I done? She felt her hand go up to her face, thick with its layer of makeup. What will he think? I'm the same. I'm no different than when he first met me. How awful. He'll have a woman, a nice, sweet, gentle wife, who will come to that shabby little door and demand to know, demand to know with her sweet defeated little eyes, who I am. Will she know about the child; will she know that there ever was a child, a child banging and slamming and shouting in baby language from behind the closet door? Mother of mercy! Patience crossed herself. It was, in that moment, as if a rubber band had been drawn back and snapped between her eyes. The ridiculousness of it all. What in the world would Jackson be doing in that same place? The house could barely have lasted, let alone Jackson's patience. He'd given up the baby, moved on, somewhere, to some godforsaken place; Jackson was sitting behind his guitar in that red shirt singing some stupid out of fashion song, probably still kept his hair long, probably had cirrhosis of the liver, probably was still as skinny as a rocking chair full of knots and rickets and poverty.

I must see him, she thought quietly. I must touch the hard grainy tips of his fingernails. I must smell the grit of the factory on his clothes and the wet wool of his muffler. I must stand at the window and watch him come winding around the corner through the bare trees, swinging that bottle; I must watch him climb the hill, I must unwind the wet woolen muffler and stand in the puddle of melted snow in my bare feet and I must reach up on the tiptoes of my boy's feet, my lean young boy, and press my tongue into the soft underside of his lip and feel his arms come around me and hold me, hold me, grind his palms into my shoulder blades; I must feel the drip of ice in his beard and tell him, my voice muffled and blurry in the slit of his lips and tongue and teeth that I love him, that I want him, that I will stay now, that I want to come back, that I didn't know then, that I know now, that we can do it now, that I will be eaten now, eat me Jackson, eat what's left of all that has been eaten up. Only be my brother. Only be my lost Octavio. Rid me of this stinking arrangement, of this human toilet that I have become. You saw me more accurately than Octavio ever did. You loved me more deeply than he ever could have. You were my brother. My true brother. You never took anything from me. Oh agony. Oh fucking agony, to come crawling out of a sewer after twenty years and know that you won't be there. Just when I realized.

Chapter Five
The Paper Towel Dispenser

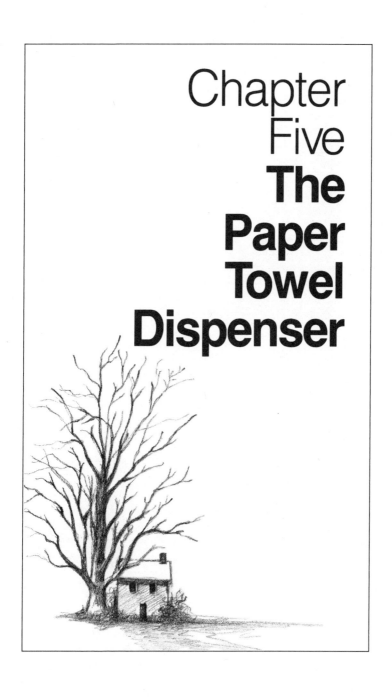

The Paper Towel Dispenser

To Frisco, the woman coming up the road was like a pebble breaking still water. He was stretched up tall and straight, his axe slung in the air, cutting wood. There were flecks of snow falling. It was an afternoon so still that Frisco saw her with a kind of astonishment, as if part of the mountainside had stirred and begun to move.

He laid down his axe. The goats came slowly out of the shed.

When she saw the goats her heart quickened with such a lurch that Patience crashed to her knees in the cinders beside the tracks. The toes of her high heels were filled with snow, and she could feel the palms of her hands crack with cold as they struck the sharp rocks. She gathered up her big vinyl purse and dug into it for a cigarette. She stood smoking in the snow by the tracks, shyly kicking at the stones, her heart thudding. She could make out the figure of the man by the shed, but she knew right away that it was not Jackson. The house seemed weary as ever, leaning a bit on one side now. Surely they couldn't be the same goats, she thought. Colina and Red Cross, the nasty one. Children of the goats, perhaps, and the man, young, perhaps a son of Jackson's. Perhaps a stranger, just a new generation of hippies, born to live in hippie houses, proud to choke every night on that chalky, cheesy goat milk. She opened her compact. She drew a sharp red line over her lips. Her ankles were freezing and her heart was broken.

They say that I am sick. Sometimes I know it, the way you know you are bleeding, the way you see blood, but there is no pain yet, and everyone is honking around you, applying pressure to someplace that bleeds but does not hurt, and they want you to be frightened, and they want you to hold still—I know my arms and legs have been in straps, but it is unreal to me, because my head is numb, because they are patching and sewing places that don't matter—sew my mother into me—that would matter. Patch the hole my father made. Tack the red shirt with seams into the flesh of my neck and arms and let me live in the texture of those years when I was self sufficient and could thrill at the aroma of wet flannel and whiskey because I did not need love, not in the years between Patience and the time when I came to look like Patience—in those in between years I only needed quiet, and I had it—all the quiet I needed—I had the river, I had the bony knobs of my knees and elbows—I had the barest memory of something missing but not too much—slight—livable—I had a greasy vinyl doll with rooted hair named Peggy—a little vinyl adult with the tits and ass of a mommy or a whore, who rode around the kitchen linoleum in a cardboard shoebox sports coupe, around the dangerous curves of my father's workboots, her hands never leaving the wheel.

Peggy. Somewhere along the line she lost her high heels, yet continued to stand on her toes.

There was a moment, standing up barechested in the back of Jackson's pick-up, when I could fling out my arms and feel completely full. The rubber bands at the tips of my braids would beat violently against my shoulder blades, and my spine would crash with every pot hole on the old river road, and my eyes would fill, with wind, or with something else—with joy—I loved being left completely alone to survive the speed and dust and trauma—the come-what-may of my father's drunken driving—the deafening roar of fenders and squealing brakes—the possibility of being thrown to my knees and the stubborn, dogged refusal to be thrown—down by the river—the refusal to be anything but happy.

Through the filthy window the back of my father's neck—ragged, the hairs fluttering up, the hollow like a wad of dead leaves—my father on the other side of glass, oblivious, the radio on.

What was my relationship to words then? It is hard to know. I may have had many words, or I may have had none. In any case I had no one to give them to. They made an odd paisley soup inside my head while Jackson tuned his guitar and sputtered the same nonsense words—*oh, hard is the fortune of all womankind; she's always controlled, she's always confined*—Jackson's face tilted up to the ceiling—his broken tooth, his gold tooth, his cracked lips—all the words came from Jackson, from behind the breastplate of his guitar, while I stirred and rattled and bled to death under the kitchen table in a blizzard of ghoulish paper dolls.

I'm not afraid of you, Jackson. Sit in my wrist if you wish, in my shoulder, my head. Sit in my crotch, rip open my eyeball, let them inject me—I'll tell the truth—the truth is that you may torture me, that you may rape and beat and murder me, but I'll find my words, I'll kill this madness long before you kill me, and for only one reason—because once, in the time after Patience, and before I came to look like Patience, I was okay, I was enough. You were on the other side of the glass.

My mother lives in the paper towel dispenser. It is a secret, kept carefully—I go into the bathroom and close the door—It is pitch black—I press my forehead against the cold steel of the paper towel dispenser and Patience is there, clogged into the metal as if it had a vein running through it—she is trapped in there—she pleads with me to come and press the shredded hole of my forehead, that she might seep in—out of the cold metal and into the hot, bloody flesh.

What does she want?

More than anything, she wants me to give her life. As if I could now employ her the way my father once did—design to make her stay—trap her in a body she does not really want—I tell her; I tell the paper towel dispenser—you don't really want me—it's an illusion of yours, based on grass you now think is greener—you don't really want me, Patience—you never did—what you want is stainless steel—to live in a stainless steel body lined with veins, encased in veins that will not flow—thanks for locking me in that closet, mother—now I watch you, I hear you howling from your prison, and I will not give you this warm, living flesh; though it aches and throbs for you I will keep it, I will guard it with the armor of the red shirt, and you will stay chained to the wall—and if they give me drugs I will tell the truth—my mother lives in the paper towel dispenser—inanimate, bolted down, and in her face I see my own face all distorted and blurred—you tell me who is insane—for in her face I see the distorted faces of everyone who has ever stood in this bathroom looking for themselves, and she has rejected them all. I will not be the one to set her free. This hole in my head is mine—my rip—my escape hatch—my humanness—my words coming now.

My words are like the great river on the other side of the hospital wall—deep, gray—full of silt and sludge.

How I love that river.

I carry the smell of the river at low tide—I will carry it with me always—it is rank as hell, like the smell at the roots of my dead father's hair—I'm sorry—sorry to be so gross—it's an anger in me now—a rage—coming like a band of angels—trumpets of rage in the paper towel dispenser—they gave me something—something is dripping slowly in my brain—there are other patients here—watching other towel dispensers, I suppose—watching TV reruns and filling up on greenish slabs of pot roast—I can barely walk when they do this to me.

   Wait. This is a pure memory of my father trudging up from the river with a cage-full of crabs, calling for me to come see them, before I looked like Patience, before I got complicated to him—when my feet were still hooves—I'll weave a basket, but don't count on it being even, my brain is fried, you should lay down they say; the shot, the shot—I can barely walk when they do this to me.

Patience stood before Frisco. He was holding the axe in one hand. The other fell open, the palm slack, a large boyish hand sticky with resin from the wood. She kept her eyes to the ground.

   "I couldn't have expected to find him here," she was saying, smoking, shivering in her ratted coat. "It was a long time ago."

   Frisco laid the axe on the ground.

   "Who are you?" he asked quietly, though already something was beginning to happen, in his temples, his throat, his chest, his eyes. Already his eyes had begun to glaze over with tears. It was the same face. No one on the earth could deny it, not see it, not be stopped as if shot with the resemblance of it under its cloud of pink and red. The wild black brow rippled like a flag, and the round harvest moon of the face warmed all the air around them.

   "I'm no one," she said quickly, taking a long drag. "He's gone, huh? I'm surprised the house still stands. When did you buy it?"

"It's not mine," Frisco said slowly. "It's his. He's gone."

Patience raised her eyes quickly.

"On the road?" she asked.

"Gone," Frisco answered, and he reached out suddenly, impulsively, and grabbed her arm. "A few days ago."

Patience looked away, down to the river. She looked for a long, long time. "Shit," she breathed, letting out a stream of smoke and cold. "Shit. Fuck."

With his free hand Frisco brushed his eyes and resettled his spectacles.

"Please," he said. "It's as if God . . ."

Patience kicked violently at the log he had been splitting and sat down on the wood stump. Crystals of ice clung to her hair.

"I know you," Frisco said. He knelt beside her. "You're her mother."

"I needed him," Patience whispered.

Chapter Six
Pia

Pia

Where did the Indians go? Like a votive candle, the question had burned inside Hannah all her life. She needed only to turn to it and it was there, the Indian question: what were they doing on hot summer days, on wet autumn nights, in blizzards, in downpours, in electrical storms—foraging—she saw them always foraging, burrowing, hustling—hungry though not unhappy, terribly uncomfortable, though not necessarily aware of it. How conscious had they been? She ached to know. Perhaps I was there, she thought, later in her life, when Jackson started to talk about something called karma—but earlier, as early as early childhood, Hannah had simply wanted to know what it had been like for them, what they had said about their love for one another, what it felt like, caring and foraging and living on the banks of the river she loved so deeply. This wondering was part of being a native, she supposed, for though Jackson had come down from New England, she had been born here, on the Hudson, had dove through its murky water with her eyes open, a sixty or seventy pound fish in search of sunken beer cans—she knew, early in her life, that the Indians would have delighted in the sparkle of beer cans in the sun, the children especially, turning in awe, speechless with joy, fawning their great brown eyelids.

"Please come in," the woman doctor said. "I'm sorry to keep you waiting so long."

Hannah rose slowly from the milk crate she had been sitting on. Her head still throbbed, the skin drawn tight, and the drugs made everything blurry and somehow suspicious. Her body was not to be trusted, not the hands or the feet, but the arms and shoulders and neck stunk with oil and sweat and the sheen of worn flannel. Spots of dried blood had crusted hard on the material.

The room was thickly carpeted and quiet. The glare of linoleum, the smell of urine, the shriek and babble of patients and nurses faded away and Hannah was suddenly happy. She crossed the room and went directly to the window where she gazed out at the sparkling black ice of the Hudson.

I would have come here a long time ago for this view, she thought.

The woman sat quietly on the edge of her desk, watching. For a moment Hannah did not turn to her.

"You mind if I smoke?" the woman asked.

Hannah did not answer.

She glanced over her shoulder. The woman had a mop of unruly curls, perhaps deliberate. She was tall and her hips spread over the edges of the desk like the haunches of a great cat. Her clothes were nubby, woolly, soft, strange. She was bent over her cigarette lighter, and when she raised her head Hannah could see that her face was heavily made up. She was a kind of woman Hannah had never seen up close. She belonged to a world Hannah had had no dealings with.

Hannah knew she should be afraid, but oddly she was not afraid of anything here anymore. She was more afraid of her own face, billowing from the paper towel dispenser box than she was of the face of this strange timeless woman, who seemed to be only in this room, as if there were no other part of her and as if she had no other purpose in her whole life than to sit and smoke and look curiously at Hannah.

"You know, kiddo," the woman said softly, "you need a bath."

Hannah smiled.

"I know that," she said.

"Are we going to be able to pry that shirt off of you?"

Hannah looked down at herself. The frayed cuffs, the buttons sewn with different colored threads, the tattered shirttails.

"The medicine is helping," the doctor said. "You're doing better. You're going to be okay. We're going to get you through this thing."

"Is it a thing?" Hannah asked quietly. "Is it called a thing that I'm in?"

The doctor smoked. "Yeah. A thing."

"My whole life."

"That's right," the doctor said softly.

"You're going to get me through it now?"

"Not this very minute. Now we deal with you taking a bath."

Hannah turned back to the window.

"Where is your father now?" the doctor asked.

Hannah did not turn from looking out at the river, but her response was immediate.

"He's on the wall over the door."

"Ready to leave at any moment, I suppose."

"Ready to run," Hannah said.

"Yes."

"He's taking care of me," Hannah said. "He loves me."

The doctor put out her cigarette. She pushed herself off the edge of the desk and walked toward Hannah, stopping halfway to the window.

"Did he take good care of you, Hannah?" she asked.

I've seen this building all my life, Hannah thought quickly. Now I'm in it. Somewhere over the clump of woods is where we are. The goats. Frisco.

"Where is Frisco?" she asked.

"I've been talking to him. He's all right. He's taking care of the house. He's very worried about you. He found you, you know."

"I was in the closet."

"Yes."

"Jackson says that when my mother left me, she put me in the closet, and then she went away. He says I looked for her for a long time. I don't remember it. I don't remember my mother. That's what you talk about here, right? Your mother and your father?"

"Right. Your mother and your father and taking a bath."

"Am I sick?"

"Yes, you are."

"What have I got?"

"What do you think? What would you call it?"

Hannah turned from the window. The woman was standing close to her, and she was not as tall now. Hannah could smell the woman. It was a smell of fabric and clean hands.

"I've got the inability to take a bath," Hannah joked, and they both laughed.

"Yes," the woman said. "You definitely have that illness."

Hannah looked down at her feet. They were encased in a thick pair of socks, men's socks. Perhaps Frisco's or Jackson's.

"Come and sit down," the woman said.

She was beckoning toward a couch and Hannah followed her. They sat on opposite ends.

"Who are you?" Hannah asked.

The doctor thought for a moment. She began to carefully push back the cuticles on each of her fingers.

"I want you to call me Pia. It's my first name, and it's improper that you should call me that, but we'll break a rule here, all right?"

Hannah looked up over the doorway. Jackson was there. He sat perched on the molding above the door, shirtless, grinning.

"What do you want?" she asked him out loud.

Pia moved closer.

"You know you really stink," she said quietly. "You stink like hell."

Hannah covered her face with her hands.

"Get him out," she whispered.

"You get him out."

"I can't."

"Tell him to go. Tell him, Jackson—"

"Shut up!" Hannah shouted.

"Tell him he's tortured you enough. Tell him you stink with him."

"He hasn't tortured me. You lie."

"I lie? He's not torturing you? Your head's not got fifty stitches in it because of him?"

Hannah began to rock back and forth. Where did the Indians go when they saw the first great wooden ship oscillating up the Hudson? Where did the shy ones go, the frightened ones? Did they go careening back into the forest never to be heard from again?

"Look," Pia said gently. "I don't want you to hate him. I'm not calling on you to hate him, or your mother. None of that. We want only one thing here. We want Hannah. We want Hannah in her own mind. Come on. Stop rocking. Look up at me."

Hannah winced at the touch of Pia's hand.

"Easy," Pia said. "Don't let the violence come. Give me the violence. Hand it over. Give me the pain. I'm not a stranger, Hannah. I know you. I've been watching you. I know what's going on. I know he's here. I know he's in your head, in the windows, in the food. I know. Listen. Here. I've got a gown. We'll take off that shirt and put on a clean gown. We'll go down the hall to the showers. I'll stay with you, I promise. I won't leave you.

No nurses. No aides. We'll put the shirt here, in the cupboard. Right here in my office. When you come to see me you can have it. You can hold it and smell it. We can talk about it. You can live without it out there. You can live for hours at a time without it, you'll see. It will be hard at first. But you can do it. You can let me be the keeper of the shirt. I'll take good care of it. I won't let anyone touch it but you. Come on. Here. Here's the gown. It's frightfully ugly, but you won't mind. You'll get free from that smelly thing."

Hannah looked up. Pia was close to her now. She looked into Pia's eyes. They said nothing to each other. Slowly, without a word, Hannah began to unbutton the red shirt. She held it close around herself, and when all the buttons were undone she folded back each side, slowly, deliberately, and closed her eyes quickly as she heard Pia gasp. She knew what Pia was seeing. The scars, hundreds and hundreds of them, round pink swollen angry red scars, with barely an inch of healthy flesh between them, spinning in circles from her nipples outward, the raised charred flesh of hundreds of cigarette butts pressed silently over the years until the skin of the breasts was mutilated beyond description, folded and pocketed and blue with damage.

When at last she opened her eyes Hannah saw Pia sitting still, her eyes full of silent tears.

Chapter Seven
The Martin

The Martin

I didn't come to see the baby, the girl, the woman. The damaged, crazy, broken woman. I didn't come to see some strangled adolescent who was going to now cling to me, who was going to have some lost mommy scene with me. Fuck you, Jackson. I didn't come to clean this up. I came for you. For you to take care of me, not for me to take care of your precious little bundle, your trap, your big idea.

Patience was staring out the kitchen window toward the river. She held a glass of whiskey. Behind her Frisco sat at the table, his long legs stretched out into the middle of the room. He picked at a button of his shirt, and his hands were trembling.

He studied the crooked black seam that ran along the back of one of her calves.

No one wore stockings like that anymore.

"Are you warm enough?" he asked meekly.

"Shut up," she responded.

116 The Red Shirt

Frisco blinked his eyes rapidly.

She stood huddled over the sink in her short fake fur coat, her high heels soaked with melted snow, and from somewhere deep within her, Frisco heard a low, mean groan. A snarl. Something that ached and raged all at once. He moved his chair back an inch. He thought vaguely about making coffee.

"Is that the Martin?" she asked.

Frisco had come from outside. His arms were loaded with logs and his beard felt stiff with ice.

"Yes."

Patience walked to the table. She sat down. She poured another shot of whiskey. All the time she was staring at the big black guitar case in the corner.

"Mercy," she muttered.

She pitched back the drink.

She hooked one leg over the opposite one and began to rock it back and forth. The heel of her shoe dropped down, exposing raw red flesh that swelled through the fabric of her hose.

"You got a light?" she asked, eyeing a box of kitchen matches only several feet away. Her voice was heavy, almost sobbing with exhaustion.

Was she hard or was she soft? Wise or stupid? Clairvoyant? Propelled here like a pea from God's slingshot? Was she here to destroy or to heal?

Frisco leaned and lit her cigarette. The house was growing dark with the storm. In the matchlight her face lit up strong and round, and the bruise at the temple was serious.

She did not meet his eyes. Instead, her gaze fell obsessively on the case.

Frisco stoked the stove. His feelings were frozen. He longed to call the hospital, get help, get advice, get somebody to tell him what to do with her. She was drunk. When he glanced over his shoulder at her he saw her own shoulders rising and falling, silent, broad as planks, strong as a single ridged yoke. And just as burdened, he thought, staring into the fire. In the flames he saw Hannah's face, distorted with screams, riddled with streams of clotting blood, screaming and screaming and screaming.

"Here!" he said quickly, leaping up, going to the corner, grabbing the case.

"Here, look at it."

He snatched it up and laid it flat in her lap.

Patience froze with surprise.

"What do you mean?" she asked, her hands shooting to the brass locks and then flitting away, splintering a long red nail.

"Open it. Go on."

Frisco lurched violently toward the table and poured himself a shot of whiskey.

Patience slumped suddenly in her chair as if the wind had been knocked out of her.

"The Martin," she whispered, and she let out a deep rasping sound, a wet smoker's cough. "The Martin. God. God."

She stared down at the box.

"I was intelligent once," she said suddenly.

Frisco stood quietly, swallowing.

"Yeah. I went to college, you know." She looked up, her eyes, thick with black pencil, taking in the cupboards, the oilcloth, the wooden countertop.

118 The Red Shirt

"We used to tell each other poems. We knew poems by heart. Listen:

> All I could see from where I stood
> Was three long mountains and a wood;
> I turned and looked another way
> And saw three islands in a bay.
> So with my eyes I traced the line
> Of the horizon, thin and fine,
> Straight around till I was come
> Back to where I'd started from;
> And all I saw from where I stood
> Was three long mountains and a wood . . .

Her voice trailed off. Her eyelids brimmed with tears and a rivulet of black ran out of the corner of one eye.

Slowly, sadly, she began to hum. In a sad, desperate singsong she repeated the lines:

"Straight 'round till I was come/Back to where I'd started from."

She sniffled, rubbing the back of her hand under her nose and smudging the blackness on her cheek with her palm.

Frisco moved to touch her, but drew back, pushing up his spectacles.

"I'm so sorry," he said.

Patience seemed not to hear. She was reaching for the locks now, snapping one back.

"Yeah. I was intelligent. I had an education. I was no ordinary whore. When I met him, you know, he knew that. He saw that right away. I spoke better then. I was hard, sure, but I read. I read everything. My people, they didn't have much interest in learning. No. They brought me up to work. Nobody encouraged me. I had to leave because of it. That's why I went to New York. Learning."

She was crying hard now, stretching around after the whiskey bottle.

"You needn't think I'm just some twat."

Frisco grabbed the bottle from her hand. He poured a shot of whiskey and then he came and knelt before her, setting the little glass in her hand.

"I don't," he said.

For the first time since they had entered the house, Patience looked at him. She reached out and drew her fingers through the full length of a strand of his golden hair.

"It's almost white in some places," she said tenderly.

"You must have loved him very much," Frisco said.

"No," she said. "I loved someone else very much." She took a drink of the whiskey. "Until now. Now I realize they were the same man. Only the first man was not real. He was . . ." She paused. "Imaginary. Jackson was really him. I just didn't know it. I didn't know it until this morning in the Chock Full O' Nuts when I was stirring a cube of sugar into my coffee." She shrugged. "I'd had a bad night."

Frisco indicated her injury with a jerk of his chin. Patience waved her hand.

"You get hurt," she said. "That's not it. Or maybe that is it. Maybe you get hurt one time too many after twenty years. Maybe you get struck by lightning. Jackson would, he would've . . ."

She bit her lip.

"He would've taken you back?" Frisco asked.

"You think so?" Patience whispered.

Frisco took the glass from her. He set it on the table, and still kneeling, he undid the locks of the guitar case. They both gazed down at the lid. Already the smell of rosewood and cedar was wafting toward them.

"Yeah," Frisco said. "You know, I think he was actually waiting for you."

Patience lifted her face to the ceiling and breathed deeply through her nostrils. Then she folded back the cover and drew out Jackson's guitar. In an instant Frisco's eyes filled with tears, and it was only through a blur that he saw her whole face transform, transform into one of the loveliest faces of a woman that he had ever seen, the tenderest, sweetest, most vulnerable, primitive, earthen face in all the world. In a flash the case clattered to the floor and she pressed the instrument to her breast, the box echoing with the touch of her hands, and her lips, full and soft and rich, pressed down hard into the ruddy red rosewood of the fingerboard.

"Oh my darling," she cried, and in her voice was ecstasy.

Frisco rose, shuffling away, frightened. He wanted so much himself to reach out and touch the thing, touch the oily smudges left on the pick guard, touch the greasy steel strings, trace the nicks of time and abuse and drunkenness, clasp the thing to his own breast, clasp them both, guitar and woman, and rock them and hold them, and cry and cry. But the guitar was hers, rightfully and forever, and, as he kicked back the door and stumbled out into the night he realized that the same was true for Hannah.

She was still holding the Martin when he came in with the evening milk. The pails were steaming, metallic smelling, and as he fussed with them over the sink he kept his back to her. She was silent now, barely stirring, and he could feel how heavy she was with sleep and whiskey.

He was hurting. He thought of Hannah, somewhere up in those rooms, hurting. They hadn't let him see her yet, but he had seen the woman doctor, he had told her everything he knew until she had leaned quietly over her desk, laying down her pencil, and demanded, "Tell me, what are your feelings for her?" Then he had stopped, stopped altogether; then he had gotten up, excused himself, muttered sorry, sorry, I can't talk to you about that.

He was hurting. Hannah was hurting. Patience, punch drunk, whiskey drunk, her cheek cushioned on the box of the guitar, was hurting.

"You should go to sleep," he said, without turning around.

"Is she like me?" Patience asked.

Frisco bristled. Until then he had thought she was barely conscious. He turned from the sink, wringing his hands. He eased himself up onto the countertop and stared at his own reflection in the black window.

"You need attention," he said. "Your head is hurt bad."

"Is she?"

Frisco paused.

"Her skin is dark like yours."

Patience considered this.

"Her hair?"

"Thick. Dark. Full of red in summer."

Patience nodded.

"Is she smart?"

"I don't know."

Frisco dipped a ladle into the milk and poured it into a cracked teacup. He got down.

"Here."

Patience looked up and sleepily made a face.

"I hate the stuff."

"It'll help you sleep."

She waved her hand.

"I'm already asleep."

Frisco set the milk down and moved to take the guitar.

"Come on."

Patience began to cry.

"Is she pretty?"

"She's beautiful."

"Does she drink?"

"Sometimes."

"When did she leave home?"

Frisco hesitated.

"She—I told you—a few days ago she was taken . . ." He took the guitar from Patience and laid it in its case. "She hasn't left," he said. "She's not a grown-up. She hasn't even finished high school. She still lives here."

Patience gasped.

"What? Here? Where?"

Frisco nodded toward the curtain. Patience spun around.

"Where is she? Jesus, man, where is she?"

She stood up.

Frisco was suddenly concerned. She seemed to have forgotten things he had told her. She was drunk. He reached out. With tender fingers he tried to touch the bruised spot on her face, but Patience drew back, baring her teeth. Frisco pressed his lips together. He reached again, but this time he touched her chin, feeling it tremble.

"I'll take you to her," he said.

"Take me right now," she demanded.

Frisco looked deeply into her eyes. For a moment he considered warming up the truck.

"It's snowing," he said. "It's night."

He took his thumb from her chin and pushed back his spectacles. "Come on. I'll show you where she sleeps. You sleep in her space tonight."

Patience looked down at her filthy coat.

"She scares me so much," she said. "God, she scares me."

It was a rag doll. Black, like a voodoo doll, with x's and o's for features, and an Aunt Jemima kerchief. It was worn, and smelled of rotted insides. Patience lay quietly on her side in the dim little room and considered this thing that lay on the pillow beside her. She was still dressed, wrapped in her coat, and burrowed beneath a pile of quilts. Deep beneath the covers she could feel that she still had her shoes on.

Slowly, like a banner unfurling, a question formed. She leaned over, and looking at the doll she whispered:

"Tell me, what did he name her?"

Her head was throbbing. She closed her eyes and slept a few more moments. Around her the room spun and spun. When she woke again there was more light.

A crude, boxy dresser with a mirror and a flat, old fashioned hairbrush. Nothing more but the books, a wall of them standing like hundreds of silent witnesses—Patience smiled, stretched, shook the little doll by the shoulder.

"She reads!" she exclaimed.

Nothing else. No picture, no rug, no lamp, knickknack, crucifix, record player. No slippers, no chair. No room to move about. Her life, her childhood, had gone on here. Patience closed her eyes. The other room, on the other side of the kitchen, she knew that room by heart. She knew the smell of the sheets and the creak of the bedsprings. She knew the rhythm of the cane bottomed rocker and the clatter of goat hooves on the rocks outside the window. She knew the silky, reedy scent of marijuana and the leathery grains of his tongue parting her vulva.

"Christ," she groaned, rolling to her back. She could feel the mascara crusted hard to her lashes. The fear of what was to come came over her in a wave of deep, determined nausea, and she leapt, quickly, clattering on her high heels for the toilet.

And then they were in the truck. Heat blasted and rattled from the box by the stick shift. Frisco cracked open his window and a strand of his hair blew up and fluttered wildly on the outside. They were both blinded by sun and snow, and the river lay like a great polished dance floor.

Patience clutched her vinyl pocketbook and stared straight ahead. She had taken great care with her face. The eyes were lined and looped and shaded in thick black charcoal. The flat wide planes of the cheeks were so deeply red that they were close to blue, and the mouth was scarlet, some cheap kind of scarlet that was already cracking in the cold. She held her head high and proud, or perhaps defiant, or perhaps delirious, and her hair raged all around her head like steel wool. The bruise was swelled brown and green with blood. She had not bathed, nor even washed her hose, and her dress, a cheap polyester mini-shift of some sort, was still splattered from the trainyard. None of this seemed to concern her. She had wrapped a newspaper around her chest under her coat, and, upon entering the cab of the truck she had immediately opened the glove box, her eyes glistening, and snatched up a pair of tattered rawhide workgloves.

Frisco, warm in his army jacket and muffler, pitied her.

He had no plan. He had not the slightest idea of

what to do. Storm the gates? Bang his way into the ward with this wild woman? Phone the woman doctor from downstairs? Would Patience stand for it? Would she wait?

"You'll have to wait," he said, clearing his throat. "They won't just let you see her. They won't let anyone see her."

Patience looked at him.

"You said you'd take me to her."

Frisco cleared his throat again.

"You'll see her doctor. She's a woman doctor. She'll talk to you. She'll tell you whether you can see her or not."

Patience snarled.

Frisco reached up and pushed back his spectacles.

"I know her. Let me tell her to let you see Hannah."

Patience did not respond. She grappled with her pocketbook and pulled out a cigarette. Suddenly, with a violent mania that caused Frisco to contract in fear, she threw back her head, and, in a voice scratchy with sleep and smoke she began to shout out old spirituals:

Go down Old Hannah!

Hurry Sundown!

Frisco braked hard and reached for a hospital parking stub.

"Quiet now," he pleaded. "Please, please God, be quiet."

She stopped as suddenly as she had started. Her eyes, gleaming out from under their paint, had begun to study the heavily barred windows of that huge brick place.

Chapter Eight
Sanity

Sanity

A few moments later, Frisco was standing before Pia. She had risen quickly, papers scattering, her eyes flashing in anger.

"What?" she demanded, and then instantly, seeing it was him, seeing him tremble, tearing at his muffler, his lips knocking against one another, stuttering, shuffling.

"Frisco!" she exclaimed, coming around the desk, swift and sturdy on her big haunches, "Jesus, what is it? What's happened?"

Patience paced the corridor. They had locked the door behind Frisco, a sick clattering of keys, and she kicked the door, hard, and spat on the floor. There was no one in the hallway. Only a bench. She sat down, hooked one leg over the other, and smoked.

"She's here," Frisco said quietly. "Her mother. Patience."

Pia whistled through her teeth and sat down on the edge of her desk. There was a long pause. She ran her fingers through her hair, lit a cigarette, drew on it, and stamped it out.

"Well," she said softly. And then, grabbing a set of keys, "I'll go out and see her. Wait here."

Frisco pushed up his spectacles. He did not sit down, but went to the window and looked out at the river.

Looking through the grate, Pia felt her stomach turn over. It was very bad. She knew that she would have to tell Hannah, that Hannah would have to make a choice whether or not to see this woman . . . but how could it be? How could the timing of life be so off, so crazy, to have delivered this person to them now, when it was all so fragile? She cursed under her breath and turned the locks.

"I'm Hannah's doctor," she said, stretching out her hand.

The woman did not meet her gaze. She was pressing out the cigarette under her shoe, muttering a little, casting around for her big broken pocketbook. Pia stared at the bruise. She could smell Patience, and it was not good.

Suddenly Patience stood up. She was smaller than Pia, despite her furry coat, but she drew herself up as high as she could. Last night's whiskey was still on her breath.

"I was looking for Jackson," she whispered. Her eyes sought Pia's, and they were like Hannah's eyes, dim, psychotic, shy, intelligent and yet damaged almost beyond all intelligence.

"He's not here," Pia said.

Patience walked away in a little circle and came back.

"Maybe she can tell me about him."

"She's not in any shape," Pia said. "She's very sick."

"She knew him. She lived with him."

"She's sick," Pia said again.

"I have a right," Patience said quickly.

"Yes, you do," Pia said. "If she consents. Only if she consents."

"She will. I'm her mother."

Pia sat down on the bench. She rested her elbows on her knees and studied the floor.

"Do you know what you're doing?" she asked. "Is it for her? Are you thinking of her? Because this is going to make her sicker. She has no memory of you. None at all. She only knows that you left her."

Patience stood over Pia.

"Let me see her face."

"Why?"

"Him," Patience muttered.

"Who?" Pia asked.

"Oct—" Patience shrugged. "Jackson."

Pia sighed and stood up. "Jackson is not in her face," she said. She tried to soften, to stand closer, but Patience inched away. "You need help," Pia said gently. "Patience, we can help you here. We have other units. You could rest, get well. After awhile you could see each other."

"Now!" Patience screamed. "Now, damn it!" And

she brought her fist up and bit the knuckle. "You tell her I'm here. You tell her her mother is here."

"And then what?" Pia whispered.

Patience stood very still. Only her eyes moved, in quick darting motions, from side to side.

"Tell her . . ." Patience grasped her big bag to her chest and chewed her lower lip. "Tell her I brought her some candy."

Pia felt her face go hot. She turned away and reached for her keys.

"I'll send Frisco out to wait with you," she said. She slid the bolt. She did not turn around. "Wait," she whispered. "I'll be back."

She found Hannah in the Occupational Therapy room, her bald head bent over a simple child's basket, her hands trembling with dim concentration.

Pia drew the therapist to one side.

"Has she spoken today?"

"Not yet."

She greeted a few of the patients who had begun to flurry around her. Hannah did not look up. Pia broke away and went to Hannah's side, pulling out a chair and easing herself down. Hannah's lips began to move, silently.

"Hannah," Pia spoke in a whisper. She touched Hannah's shoulder and was relieved when Hannah did not wince or draw away. "Will you come to my office?"

Hannah looked up and her thick bushy eyebrows, which had been furrowed in concentration, smoothed out into a question.

"Yes," Pia nodded, "you can see the shirt."

Hannah stood up.

"But there's something else," Pia said quickly.

"Something's happened, and you've got to talk to me. We've got to talk. Tell me now that you will talk."

Hannah looked down at the little basket.

Pia reached and touched it.

"It's pretty, Hannah," she said. "You're doing so well. Someday you're going to tell me all about this basket, right? Tell me where you'll put it when you take it home."

Hannah looked up, out over the heads of the other patients.

"Don't make me go," she whispered.

"Oh, no!" Pia exclaimed, laughing. "Not just yet. Not for a long time, right?"

"Right," Hannah said.

In the office Hannah went immediately to the cupboard, pulling back the door, leaning in and snatching up the red shirt. She held it to her cheek. She smiled. Pia put her arm around Hannah's shoulder.

"Listen to me, Hannah. There's someone here to see you, but you don't have to see her if you don't want to. We're going to talk about it. You're going to make a choice."

Hannah stiffened. How could she know, Pia thought, amazed, uttering a little cry, almost of horror, for in that instant she knew that Hannah knew. How was it possible, and yet here it was, here was Hannah, going to the window, clutching the shirt, shaking her battered head slowly from side to side.

"We'll get you some extra medication," Pia said, staring at the back of her.

"No," Hannah said.

"Frisco is here," Pia said. "Would you like to see him?"

"No," Hannah said.

"He loves you very much, Hannah."

"Yes," Hannah said.

"Then will you let him—"

"No."

Pia edged her way closer.

"What do you want to do?"

Hannah looked down. She wore a plain scrub suit and her feet were bare. She slid one big toe over the soft carpet.

"Barefoot is against the rules," she said.

"Shall I send her away?" Pia asked.

"No," Hannah said.

"What then?"

Hannah turned around. Her eyes were strangely clear, calm. "Take me to the door," she said. "And slide back the shutter at the grate. I want to look at her."

Pia marvelled at this. Her hand went nervously to her throat.

"Okay," she said. "Come."

They went down the long yellow tunnel of the corridor, past the bright blue line that patients were not allowed to cross, to the great steel door, painted battleship gray, peeling in places.

"I'm going to go through and tell them what you want," Pia said. "And then I'll be right back."

Hannah nodded. She was holding the red shirt to her heart now, and her hands were trembling terribly.

Pia resisted her doubts. She turned the key and disappeared.

In a moment she was back.

"All right," she said tensely. "We'll slide the shutter."

Hannah pulled herself up to the grate. She looked silently out into the other corridor.

Patience was standing over by the bench, and when the shutter slid back she looked up, bleary eyed, and stumbled toward the barred window. She gazed at the bald, stitched skull, at the wild, rough brow, so like her own, and at the flat, round, moonshaped face. Her scarlet mouth dropped slightly open. Her eyes rolled up.

Hannah saw her mother begin to swoon, and then catch herself. She saw her bring a handful of crusted red nails up to the thick glass as if to touch her. She saw the bruise and the layers of paint, and the droop of the heavy, awful lips. She saw eyes that would not focus. Eyes that would never see her. She saw her drunken, ravaged mother, and, in a corner over her mother's shoulder she saw Frisco, fixed in shock. She drew slowly away from the window. Pia was bending over her in concern. Hannah turned the red shirt over in her hands. She pressed her nose into the collar. She looked up at Pia.

"Take it out to her. Give it to her."

She pushed the shirt into Pia's breast. She began to walk away.

She heard Pia turn the key.

Later she lay very still on her bed while Pia gave her an injection. She felt Pia's big hands move gently over her back, massaging the shoulder blades. The trembling began to ease, the voices grew quieter. She lay under Pia's hands, numb, aware of Jackson, somewhere, going out, out like the tide of the river, out in the distorted arms of her mother, being carried away like trash, debris . . .

Where had her father come from? He never said. She knew he had been born in New England and had traveled down to the river when New York was the place for folksingers. But who had been Jackson's mother, his father? Who had he loved before Patience? She would never know now, for Jackson was going out of her, the medicine was carrying him out, and he would not be back, except in dreams, and the dreams would always be fuzzy and confused and untouchable.

"You know, kiddo," Pia whispered, "this is the beginning of sanity."

Hannah lay very still. "It's very hard," she whispered sleepily.

"It's the hardest thing there is," Pia said.

And Hannah put her face into the pillow, feeling the heat and the weight and the deep silty salt of tears, beginning; she was at the very beginning, and she began to sob with all her heart.